MOLLY MALO... ...AM STOKER IN

DOUBLE TROUBLE. AT THE DEAD ZOO

'This book is a gem from start to finish, packed with
laughs, thrills and characters that sparkle on the page.
My new favourite double act – smarter than Holmes
and Watson and much funnier.'

Eoin Colfer, author of the Artemis Fowl *series*

ALAN NOLAN grew up in Windy Arbour, Dublin and now lives in Bray, Co. Wicklow with his wife and three children. This is Alan's second book about Molly Malone and Bram Stoker; their first adventure is *Molly Malone and Bram Stoker in The Sackville Street Caper*. Alan is the author and illustrator of *Fintan's Fifteen*, *Conor's Caveman* and the *Sam Hannigan* series, and is the illustrator of *Animal Crackers: Fantastic Facts About Your Favourite Animals*, written by Sarah Webb. He runs illustration and writing workshops for children, and you may see him lugging his drawing board and pencils around your school or local library.

www.alannolan.ie

Twitter: @alnolan

Instagram: @alannolan_author

MOLLY MALONE & BRAM STOKER IN

DOUBLE TROUBLE. AT THE DEAD ZOO

ALAN NOLAN

THE O'BRIEN PRESS
DUBLIN

This edition first published 2023 by
The O'Brien Press Ltd,
12 Terenure Road East, Rathgar,
Dublin 6, D06 HD27, Ireland.
Tel: +353 1 4923333; Fax: +353 1 4922777
E-mail: books@obrien.ie
Website: obrien.ie

The O'Brien Press is a member of Publishing Ireland
ISBN: 978-1-78849-434-2

Layout and design by Emma Byrne
Cover illustration by Shane Cluskey
Internal illustration p239 by Shane Cluskey
Map, posters and internal chapter header illustrations by Alan Nolan
Author photograph p2 by Sam Nolan
All rights reserved.

8 7 6 5 4 3 2 1
26 25 24 23

Printed and bound in Great Britain by Clays Ltd, Elcograf S.p.A.
The paper in this book is produced using pulp from managed forests

Published in

DEDICATION

For the Mangled Ferrets

TABLE OF CONTENTS

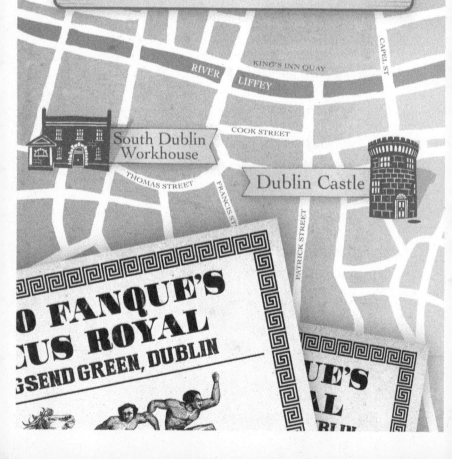

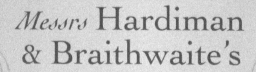

Messrs Hardiman & Braithwaite's

Patented Map *of* Dublin City

1858

Updated Edition 1859

RIVER LIFFEY

KING'S INN QUAY

CAPEL ST

COOK STREET

South Dublin Workhouse

THOMAS STREET

FRANCIS ST

Dublin Castle

PATRICK STREET

O FANQUE'S
CUS ROYAL
G SEND GREEN, DUBLIN

UE'S
AL
BLI

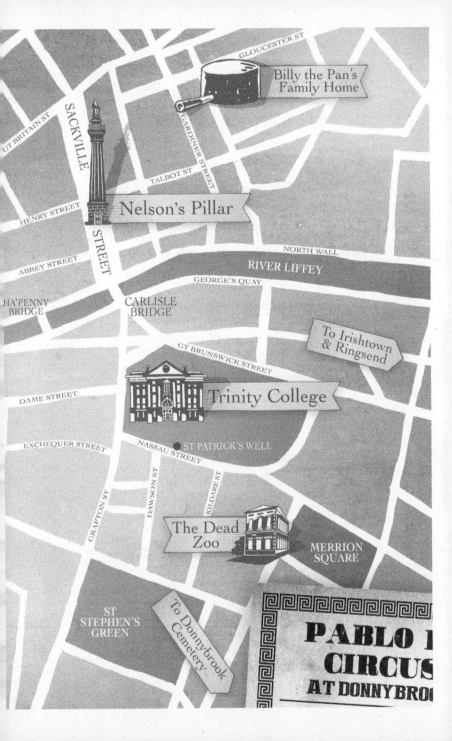

A Short List of Characters Contained Within, Provided by the Most Considerate Author for Your Instruction and Delight:

Bram Stoker

The future author of *Dracula*, almost twelve years of age, yearns for adventure and to have stories to tell.

Molly Malone

Twelve years of age, accomplished sneak thief and part-time fishmonger.

Shep, Rose, Billy the Pan, Calico Tom, aka The Sackville Street Spooks

Molly's gang, to whom she is part sergeant major, part mother hen.

Sanjit Chandra

A young boy visiting from Bombay in India, Sanjit is shy, but very clever.

Uncle Seth Kumar

Sanjit's uncle, a professor of Animal Biology at the University of Calcutta.

Hetty Hardwicke

Molly's competition for the title of best sneak thief in Dublin and self-proclaimed leader of The Bow Street Bowsies.

Madame Florence Florence

A fortune teller, variously known as the Seer of the What-Is-To-Come, the One Who Knows All, the Seventh Daughter of a Seventh Daughter, and the White Witch of Westmoreland Street.

Mr Bertram 'Wild Bert' Florence

A semi-retired Wild West trick-rider, zebra-wrangler and pony-vaulter, and Madame Flo's husband.

Mr Pablo Fanque

British owner of Pablo Fanque's Circus Royal, and sometime benefactor of Mr Bertram 'Wild Bert' Florence.

Mr Abraham Stoker & Mrs Charlotte Stoker

Bram's father and mother – his father is a strait-laced civil servant and Keeper of the Crown Jewels at Dublin Castle; his mother is a skilled story-teller and incurable chatterbox.

HOME SWEET HOME?

A lamplighter strolled from lamppost to lamppost in the evening gloom, touching the crown of each with the flame at the top of his malacca cane pole until the gas ignited and the lantern glowed with yellow radiance. He whistled a cheery tune through his bushy whiskers as he walked, leaving a line of luminous puddles of light along the length of Buckingham Street. To Bram, gazing down from his third-storey bedroom window, the rings of amber lamplight looked like ghostly stepping-stones. He imagined leaping from his window and bouncing from one light to the other, until he was away and free, and had left 19 Buckingham Street far behind. Oh, Buckingham Street was fine in its way, but it didn't feel like *home*.

Pulling the wooden shutters across and turning from the window, Bram struck a long, tapered match and carefully lit the candle on his bedside table. *Hmmmm*, he thought, looking at the ceramic candlestick in the shape of a red-coated soldier and wrinkling his freckled nose slightly, *I really must get rid of that childish thing; I am almost a man now – well, a young man, at any rate! – and young men most definitely don't need to be guarded by red-coated soldiers, ceramic or otherwise, while they sleep.*

Bram plucked the candlestick soldier from the locker and, holding it aloft, ran the candle's flickering light along the row of books on the mahogany shelf above his bed. Books by Herman Melville – *Moby-Dick* was his favourite – Edgar Allan Poe, Alexandre Dumas, and of course, his beloved Charles Dickens. Sitting in pride of place on the shelf was Bram's most treasured book, in fact his most treasured *possession*: the leather-bound copy of *A Christmas Carol*, signed for him by Mister Dickens himself! Bram smiled softly as he remembered the night in the Rotunda Round Room when he met the celebrated author and received the book, his smile growing more wistful as he recalled who he was with when that happened.

Taking the book down from the shelf, he sat on his bed and stared at the great man's signature. *Shall I ever be a famous author too,* he thought, *just like Mr Dickens? I should so very much like to be!*

He wondered where his friend Molly Malone was now — still in America, he supposed. But what was she doing? What adventures was she having? And with whom? Did she ever think of him?

Sighing sharply, he stood and replaced the Dickens book and took down another leather-bound volume, its cover more battered and worn than the pristine jacket of *A Christmas Carol*. Sitting down again on his single bed, Bram opened his old, much-used and much-loved diary, slid the pencil out from between its pages, and began to write.

The Diary of Master Abraham Stoker

Friday 18th of March, 1859

19 Buckingham Street, Dublin

Dearest Diary,

I never thought I'd say this, and I shall deny it if you mention it to anybody, but ... I miss Marino Crescent. I know this new house in Buckingham Street is much grander — it has more storeys and larger rooms. And a bigger kitchen. Wood-panelled walls too. And is exceedingly more befitting a gentleman like my father who works, as he does, in the lofty position of the Keeper of the Crown Jewels at Dublin Castle.

But it's draughty and cold, even in March. It's not small and cosy like our lovely little house in Clontarf. But it is closer to the City, and closer to Dublin Castle with Papa's precious Crown Jewels.

And speaking of the Crown Jewels ... I can't help asking myself where Molly might be.

It's been almost seven months since I last saw her — that's over half a year, Dear Diary — and, I have to say, life is so BORING without her.

I go to the (famously dreary) Rev. Woods' School every morning – BORING. (Thank goodness that next week is midterm break, I think I should absolutely lose my wits if I didn't have the week off.)

I am brought by Mama and Papa to fine hotels and restaurants for afternoon tea each weekend – BORING.

I spend every weeknight doing my homework and reading books – BORING. (Well, the reading books part I love, it's just the homework that practically sends me into a coma.)

I long for adventure. I crave excitement – I want so much to be an author and write books when I am older, but how am I ever to become a writer if my life lacks adventure and excitement? I practically yearn for the thrill of being chased by vicious villains intent on causing me harm.

In short, I miss being one of The Sackville Street Spooks.

I miss Molly.

What would I give, Dear Diary, to hear a jolly knock at the hall door, to look out of my bedroom window and see, far below, a curly mop of red hair on top of a faded blue dress and a grubby pinafore?

But ... that's just the merest flight of fancy on my behalf. You see, we are not in Marino Crescent anymore – if Molly did come back, I expect she wouldn't be able to find me.

I think that's the real reason I dislike 19 Buckingham Street so much; Molly doesn't know that I live here.

Till BORING old tomorrow, Dear Diary,

Bram

CHAPTER ONE

GUESS WHO'S BACK, BACK AGAIN, MOLLY'S BACK, TELL A FRIEND

IN WHICH A RUDDY-HAIRED ROVER RETURNS, AND BRAM SETS OFF FOR THE LATE-NIGHT CITY SIGHTS

Bram placed his pencil inside the pages of his diary and set it down beside the soldier candlestick on his bedside table. After a few seconds of deliberation, he took down his copy of *Moby-Dick* from the shelf and got into bed to read. He managed almost forty full minutes of reading before he nodded off, sitting up, with the copy of Melville's book lying open and limp on his blanketed lap.

He was startled back into consciousness, he thought, by the BONGG-ing sound of the grandfather clock in the hallway striking midnight, three storeys below. *Funny.* He had been sleeping in the new house for almost four months and the grandfather clock's BONGG-ing had never woken him before.

Then he heard a different sound; to Bram it sounded almost like the sound of knuckles rapping on glass. He sat up straight, suddenly wide awake, his copy of *Moby-Dick* sliding off his bedclothes and hitting the bedroom rug with a muffled THUNKK. There it was again, the rapping noise; it *was* the sound of someone knocking on the glass window – two quick raps, then one slow. Strange how it reminded Bram of a whistle he had once heard: two high notes and one low, a whistle so ear-piercing that even the memory of it made Bram's hands move involuntarily towards his ears. *Hold on … two quick, one slow: two high, one low – that's MOLLY'S WHISTLE!*

Bram launched himself out of bed and padded quickly but quietly to the window. He hurriedly yanked the shutters open and found himself face-to-face with a very familiar set of features: two sparkling, mischievous green eyes, a freckle-covered nose and chin, and above all of that, gleaming in the moonlight, a bird's nest of unruly ginger hair.

'MOLLY!' whisper-shouted Bram, his eyes wide and his mouth hanging open in astonishment.

'Open the window and let me in, you eejit, yeh,' mouthed Molly Malone from the other side of the glass.

Bram, his eyes still comically wide, did as he was bidden, sliding up the sash window to reveal Molly Malone herself, clinging nonchalantly to the third-storey stone windowsill. Molly swung her legs around the sill and slipped into the room, landing noiselessly on the red, Chinese-patterned rug. She turned around slowly, taking in her surroundings as she brushed dust from her knee-length dark-green satin dress. She whistled quietly. Bram looked out the window and then went back to gaping at Molly. She looked different than he remembered: yes, she still had the same bird's nest of frizzy red hair and the same freckles, but her clothes were much less ragged than before. In fact, now that he looked at it, the bottle-green dress she was wearing had no tears, marks or smudges on it at all – such a change from the faded blue dress and shabby pinafore he was used to seeing her in. Some might say that her new rig-out looked almost *fashionable*. Bram looked away from her dress and went back to gaping at the window, wondering dimly how she had gotten up to his bedroom window; the bedroom was three floors up, after all!

'Well,' said Molly, sitting primly on Bram's bed, 'this is comfy.' She picked up his copy of *Moby-Dick* from the floor, glanced at the cover and put it on top of his diary on the bedside table. 'Hah! I was reading that book on the way back from America. I had to stop though; I kept havin' dreams of the ship being attacked by whales. I thought I was Captain Ahab!'

Bram finally managed to close his mouth. He blinked his eyes, shook his head and launched him-self at Molly, enveloping her in a huge, happy bear-hug. Molly, Bram's arms tight around her, struggled off the bed. 'Get away from me, ya sap,' she giggled, hugging Bram just as tight.

'What,' began Bram, staggering back and smiling incredulously, 'how …'

'Never mind that now,' said Molly, 'Come on, Quality, let's go out on the town – the night is young – besides, I haven't been to see Billy the Pan or Shep, or Calico Tom yet!'

She hasn't been to see any of The Sackville Street Spooks yet – her own gang? thought Bram. *Molly came to see me first!* He shook his head again in astonished delight.

Grabbing Bram by the hand, Molly made her way towards the bedroom door and the stairs beyond. 'Mol, aren't we … are we not leaving by the window?' asked Bram.

'The window?' whispered Molly with a grin, 'It was easy enough for *me* to get up here, me bein' the best sneak thief in Dublin an' all that; but Bram, you strike me as more of a walkin'-down-the-stairs-an'-leavin'-by-the-front-door sort of person, if ya don't mind me sayin'.'

Bram didn't mind her saying in the least bit. *I don't know how she got up that wall at all*, he thought as he stared at his friend, *she must be part bluebottle on her mother's side.* 'Oh! Hold on until I get dressed,' he whispered, a huge grin on his face, 'Turn around, please!' Molly turned her back and studied the chintz, flamingo-patterned bedroom wallpaper while Bram grabbed clothes from the end of his bed and put them on.

'Quite right,' she said in a pretty passable imitation of an upper-class Dublin accent, 'one simply mustn't visit the City in one's pyjamas!'

Giggling softly, the two friends descended the stairs as silently as they could, Bram touching Molly gently on the shoulder and mouthing a mute warning to watch the squeaky fourth step on the second flight. They tip-toed extra quietly past Bram's parents' bedroom and padded across the black and white chequered floor tiles of the high-ceilinged entrance hall. A tall front door stood at the end, the semi-circular glass window above it throwing a mix of white moonlight and yellow gaslight across the tiles. Bram lifted the latch and opened the door, glad that the handyman had oiled the creaky hinges only the week before. The cool night air hit his face, and a second later a fast-moving, furry missile hit his mid-riff, causing him to take a step back into the hallway. The missile danced around Bram on its hind legs like a shaggy-haired prima-ballerina, excitedly trying to jump up high enough to lick his face.

'Her Majesty!' cried Bram softly, 'Oh, it's so good to see you, girl!' He bent and hugged the brown bundle of fur as the happy dog yapped enthusiastically ... and loudly. 'Shush now, Her Majesty; you'll wake up the whole street with your racket, and, more importantly, Mama and Papa!'

Molly grinned and hugged both the dog and Bram tightly. 'Right,' she said, letting go and standing back. 'Master, your carriage awaits.' She swept her arm expansively towards the kerb, where standing on the cobblestones was a black Hansom cab, its driver smiling and tipping the brim of his black top hat with a leather-covered finger. The cab's large brown horse whinnied gently, allowing clouds of steam to escape from its flared nostrils.

'Since when does Molly Malone travel by Hansom cab?' asked Bram, climbing into the passenger seat and reaching down to offer a hand to his friend.

'Why, kind sir, since I became an all-American lady of leisure!' laughed Molly, whooshing Her Majesty up into the carriage and then swinging in after her.

Bram sighed and shook his head, 'Oh, Molly, I do hope you haven't sold ALL of the Crown Jewels – Papa still thinks the ones in the strongroom of Dublin Castle are the real thing – if he knew we had replaced them with gold-painted tin and fake gem-stones made of coloured glass he should be struck down with an attack of brain fever. He *is* meant to be the Keeper of the Crown Jewels, after all!'

'Don't worry, Bram,' said Molly, 'your father's job is safe and sound.' She reached down and took a familiar-looking carpet bag from the floor of the cab, plonked it on her knee and opened it. 'See,' she whispered, 'here they are, as fine and dandy as the day we borrowed them.' Bram looked into the bag; the priceless emeralds, rubies and diamonds glittered in the gaslight of the streetlamps as the carriage began its juddering journey towards Sackville Street. Bram exhaled heavily. 'Thank goodness,' he phew-ed in relief, 'they are all still in one piece!'

'Well,' said Molly, 'one or two very, very small dia-

monds may have fallen off by – a-hem – accident …'
Bram's eyebrows shot up in alarm. 'But don't worry,
Quality! I replaced them with very high-quality glass
replicas! We will soon get the real jewels back into
the Tower, chuck out the fake ones, and your papa
will never notice that they were gone at all!' Molly
closed the bag and settled back in her seat. 'Anyway,
Rose and I had to pay for our trip to America *some-
how*. And we had to provide for the rest of The Sackville Street Spooks who stayed behind.'

'Oh, yes,' said Bram; he couldn't help smiling at
his friend, 'how are the Spooks? I haven't seen them
since before you and Rose went away.'

'No,' replied Molly with a wink, 'but they've seen
you! I asked Billy the Pan and Shep to keep an eye on
you while I was away; just to make sure you didn't
get into any trouble. Any *more* trouble, I mean! How
do you think I found you so quickly in your new
house?'

'You mean The Sackville Street Spooks have been
secretly watching me the whole time?' asked Bram.
He looked out through the back window of the cab,
half-expecting to see Shep or Billy or Calico Tom

sneaking from lamppost to lamppost in their wake.

'Not so much watching you as *watching out* for you,' said Molly, giving him a light punch on the arm, 'You're one of us, Bram, a Sackville Street Spook. And Spooks look out for each other!'

CHAPTER TWO:

HOME *STREET* HOME!

IN WHICH BILLY THE PAN AND SHEP COME FACE–TO–FACE WITH
A PRETENDER TO MOLLY'S THRONE, AND MOLLY GOES FOR A
MOONLIGHT GALLOP

RATTTT-TATT! RRATTT-A-TAT-TAT!
The man finished rapping on the side
of the saucepan and swayed slightly in the smoky
Dublin air. 'There you go, Billy!' he said, holding out
a coin in his hand. Billy the Pan reached his scrawny
arm up from where he was sitting and took the

27

proffered halfpenny, making it swiftly disappear into one of the many pockets in his tattered, patched-up grey trousers. 'Thank you, sir,' he chirped, raising the battered saucepan that he wore on his head by the handle, 'and may the Luck of the Saucepan go with yeh!' The man grinned a green-toothed grin, hiccupped and staggered off.

Shep plonked himself down on the ground beside his friend and wiped his dribbling nose with the back of his hand. 'I wish I had a gimmick like yours, Billy,' he said, 'Wearing that saucepan on your head and charging everyone a ha'penny to knock on it for luck is going to make you a fortune – you're going to be rich!'

'Well, Shep,' said Billy, leaning back on a stone column and putting his hands behind his head, 'maybe when you're twelve like me you'll find your own way of standing out from all the other Beggarmen in Dublin, just like I do. Maybe when you're older like I am, you might even be invited to join the Brotherhood of Beggarmen!'

'And Beggarwomen,' squeaked a voice from behind the column. 'And Beggarwomen,' repeated

Billy with a sigh, 'Thanks for reminding me of that, Fran.' A young girl with dirty blonde hair stuck her head around the pillar and grinned at the two boys, 'No bother!' she chirped, 'Just don't forget us ladies – we can be Beggarmen too! I mean, a-hem, Beggarwomen too!' She wrinkled her nose, sniffed and disappeared again around the column.

Billy stood up from where he was sitting on the steps of the Bank of Ireland and gazed across the wide plaza of College Green. The windows set in the regal façade of Trinity College were all dark, with no candles burning behind them – nobody was studying this late in the evening. Above the closed and locked grand entrance, Trinity's triangle-shaped stone pediment gleamed white in the moonlight.

Billy the Pan wasn't fond of plying his begging trade this side of the River Liffey – he was normally on the Northside, working a patch that stretched from Sackville Street up to Montgomery Street, the infamous Monto area – but the rules of the Brotherhood of Beggarmen said that no beggar should work the same patch for more than three days at a time. He had spent the last three days north of the Liffey; it was now his turn to work the Southside. Billy was a beggarman like his father before him, and his father's father too; he knew the rules and respected them. But for some reason the Quality, the rich Dubliners in their top hats and velvet jackets and frilly frocks and petticoats, didn't seem to be as generous and *give-ish* on the Southside as they were on the North. He had to rely on the kindness of working-class people, wandering home, worse-for-wear, from public houses – *they* seemed happy enough to throw him a coin and knock on his battered saucepan for luck. Unfortunately, that meant having to stay up late until the public houses pulled down the shutters, and Billy didn't like working the late shift.

Nearly time to head home, thought Billy, *the hour is late, and College Green is nearly empty; only a few cabs goin' up and down, and the odd eejit stumblin' though – there won't be any more rappin' on my saucepan tonight!*

'C'mon, Shep,' he said, turning to his fellow Sackville Street Spook, 'I think we'll call it a night and head back to Madame Flo's.' Shep suddenly jumped to his feet, his eyes wide, nearly knocking Billy over. He pointed a shaking hand toward the stone plinth in the middle of the plaza. On the top of the plinth sat a huge bronze statue of a horse, and on top of the horse sat a huge bronze statue of King William III.

'King Billy? What's up with aul' William the Third?' asked Billy.

'Not the statue, Billy, look who's at the bottom of it!' exclaimed Shep. Walking around the side of the plinth, silhouetted by dim gaslight, was the person Shep was gesturing at. A girl with wild, bushy hair, wearing a ragged dress and pinafore. A small, furry, knee-high dog followed behind her. 'And ... is that Her Majesty too?' gasped Shep, 'It couldn't be ...'

'MOLLY MALONE!' shouted Billy. They both ran wildly down the steps of the Bank and across the cobblestones towards the small silhouette with the smaller canine silhouette beside her, but each came to a screeching halt as they saw the mysterious figure's face.

'Hold on,' cried Billy the Pan, disappointment in his voice. 'You're not Molly!'

Shep pointed at the dog, a scruffy-looking mutt with ratty brown fur and a snaggle-toothed face that looked nothing like Molly's dog, 'And this dog is just too plain ugly to be Her Majesty!'

The dog's furious furry eyebrows knitted together, and he let out what sounded like a disgusted growl of disdain.

'Hetty Hardwicke's the name,' proclaimed the girl in an imperious voice, tossing her dirty brown fuzz of hair over her shoulder contemptuously, 'and this is my dog, Prince Albert.' The small, spiky-haired dog growled again and bared his yellow teeth.

'Forget about Molly Malone; she's old news,' snarled Hetty Hardwicke, baring her own teeth just like Prince Albert. 'She up and left for Amer-i-kay *months* ago. I'm taking over her business interests here in Dublin City; me and my gang, the Bow Street Bowsies. *I'm* the best sneak thief in Dublin now that Molly's gone. And let's face it, fellas, I'll be the best for a long time to come because Molly is *never* coming back!'

'Molly *is* back,' said a familiar voice. Shep and Billy turned. Walking towards them down the steps of the bank was a girl dressed in a bright blue dress with a starched, perfectly ironed, brilliant-white pinafore. Her newly-washed hair was curly and red as it shone in the moonlight.

'Molly … Malone?' said Hetty in a small, disappointed voice. Prince Albert lowered his head and whimpered.

'ROSE!!' cried Billy and Shep in delight. They ran and hugged their old friend tight, 'You're back!'

'Back from the good old US of A! Can I get a big ol' YEE-HAAWW, fellers?' laughed Rose.

'YEEE-HAWWWW!' shouted Billy and Shep together, their voices ringing across College Green.

'I loved being in America,' said Rose, giving Shep a quick, tight hug and rapping her knuckles on Billy's saucepan hat, 'but it's great to be back home – with my family.' The three friends hugged again.

'How sweeeeeeet …' sneered Hetty in a sing-song voice, 'But you're not Molly Malone! Molly's deserted all of you, and guess what? *I'm* the top dog in Dublin now!' Prince Albert, a bit put out that she didn't think *he* was the top dog, looked up at his mistress and whined.

Suddenly three ear-splitting whistles pierced the night air, echoing back from the cold stone facades of the Bank of Ireland and Trinity College: two high whistles and one low. Hetty's face scrunched up with the noise and she put her grubby fingers into her grimy ears, but Billy and Shep's faces lit up with joy.

'MOLLY!!' squealed Shep in delight.

The real Molly Malone hopped down from the step of the Hansom cab, petted the horse and threw a coin to the driver. Bram followed her onto the cobblestones, carefully lifting Her Majesty onto the ground. 'And Bram and Her Majesty too!' added Billy the Pan, beaming.

'So ...' said Molly, winking at her friends, and then turning a hard glare in Hetty's direction, 'what's this I hear about me being losing my crown as best sneak thief in Dublin?'

Hetty stared incredulously at Molly and gulped. 'B-but ...' she stammered, 'but I thought you were gone for good ... I thought The Sackville Street Spooks were over!'

'I am afraid you seem to have been labouring under a misapprehension,' said Bram.

Hetty looked puzzled, *misapprehension*? 'I – I'm sorry – under a *what*?'

'He means,' said Molly, jutting out her freckled chin and furrowing her eyebrows, 'that Molly Malone is back in Dublin, and The Sackville Street Spooks are back in business!' As one, Rose, Shep and Billy the Pan stepped up behind Molly and Bram. Her Majesty growled a low growl at Prince Albert, her hackles rising. Hetty took a step backwards and grabbed her dog by his frayed leather collar.

'C'mon, Prince Albert,' she said, her voice quivering with anger, 'we are going – for now; but we'll be back, you can bet on it …' She threw back her bushy brown hair with as much dignity as she could muster and dragged the whimpering dog away up Church Lane.

Molly waited patiently until sound of Hetty Hardwicke's footsteps (and the sound of Prince Albert's pathetic whining) couldn't be heard anymore, then she turned to her friends, smiling broadly.

'MOLLY!!' they cried and ran to embrace her and Bram. Her Majesty skipped around the group, bouncing up and down like she had springs attached to her furry paws.

'The Sackville Street Spooks,' said Rose, through happy tears, 'back together at last!'

* * *

They walked together down Westmoreland Street, and across the Carlisle Bridge over the murky, slow-moving waters of River Liffey, until they reached Sackville Street. 'Now I really feel like I'm home,' said Molly, looking up at the huge stone column of Nelson's Pillar, outlined in pure black against the dark blue night sky, 'It only seems like yesterday when we were all here together, robbing rich people and causing mayhem ...'

Sackville Street was the area that gave The Sackville Street Spooks their name. Said to be the widest main thoroughfare of any capital city in Europe, this broad boulevard was where the young gang of pickpockets moved like unseen spectres amongst the rich and well-to-do of Dublin, pinching their purses and pilfering their pound notes. The Spooks were seldom noticed because the Quality never wanted to acknowledge the poor or the needy – the rich always turned their faces away from poverty and any sort of unpleasantness. The Spooks used that to their advantage; if the rich won't look, then the poor can slip by unnoticed, helping themselves to an odd pocket watch or an expensive (and remarkably re-sellable) silk handkerchief or two as they go.

Suddenly, they heard the sound of panicked shouting coming from the direction of Rutland Square, followed by the wild, thunderous din of hooves clattering over cobblestones. A dark shape was hurtling straight toward them through the gaslit gloom – a pitch-black carriage bouncing along crazily, being pulled by a ferocious black horse. The beast was enormous with a madly flowing mane of coarse hair, and its skin was slick with sweat. As the monstrous shape passed noisily under the dim glow of the gaslights, the friends could see white froth streaming from its muzzle. The horse bore down on them, its eyes fierce, feral and senseless. Steam seemed to be erupting from its flared nostrils into the cold air. A man clutching a battered top hat sprinted behind the runaway carriage, 'Look out!' he shouted, 'A stray cat's scared me horse – she's gone mad!'

'Get behind the pillar, all of you,' said Molly, standing out in front of her friends and gesturing with her arm.

'What are you going to do, Molly?' asked Bram his voice low and alarm in his eyes.

'That horse is spooked,' she said, her eyes on the oncoming mass of black wood, muscle and metal hurting towards her at breakneck speed, 'and I'm just the Spook to calm her down.'

Bram dragged Her Majesty around the side of the Pillar and out of harm's way. The small hound strained against the leash, barking and whining, her brown doggy eyes on the out-of-control horse and carriage rushing straight towards her mistress.

Molly stood in the centre of Sackville Street, directly in the carriage's path, her hands on her hips as if daring the horse to trample her. The noise of hooves and carriage wheels on the cobblestones was deafening and Bram held his hands over his ears as he gaped out from behind the pillar at the madly rushing horse and at Molly standing defiantly in front of it.

'Be careful, Mol!' called Rose, appearing beside him, 'remember what Little Feather taught you!' Molly glanced over and nodded quickly.

Just as the horse reached the spot where Molly stood, she deftly sidestepped out of the way. Spinning on her heel in a pirouette worthy of a ballet dancer, she reached out her arm and hooked her small hand into the horse's leather bridle. Using the momentum of the charging animal as it stormed past her, she swivelled her body around again, and in one swift move swung herself up and onto the horse's broad back. Bram, watching from the side of the pillar, gasped while the other Spooks cheered.

The huge animal's back was slippery with sweat and Molly dug her feet into the horse's sides so she wouldn't slide off. Hanging onto the beast's mane with one hand, Molly grabbed the loose reins with the other and pulled them back sharply. 'Woah!' she shouted, in a firm but kindly voice. The horse turned its huge head to look back at its unexpected rider, its eyes frightened and panic-stricken, foam flying from its muzzle. 'It's alright, girl,' said Molly, leaning towards the horse's ear. Her voice was gentle and almost a whisper, 'The moon is pale and high, and the crow sleeps; so should you, so should you.' The horse slowed a little, its hooves crashing down at a slower pace. Molly leaned further in, 'Sleep, beautiful girl, sleeeeeeeeep.'

The colossal animal slowed to a canter, then a walk, finally coming to a complete halt just before the bridge. It bent its head low towards the ground, panting. Molly slipped down off the horse's back and stroked its huge black neck. The horse continued breathing heavily in shuddering breaths, but it turned back towards the Pillar when Molly gently tugged its reins. The Sackville Street Spooks ran down the cobblestoned street to Molly, joined by a group of goggle-eyed onlookers, all of whom had witnessed the amazing spectacle.

'Is that Molly Malone?' shouted one man, wearing a leather apron with cobbler's tools in pockets at the front.

'It is!' shouted another.

'Molly's back!' the crowd cheered, 'Good on yeh, Molly!'

An old lady wearing a shabby dress waved her hat, 'Good ol' Molly Malone – she's come back to us again, thanks be!'

Molly smiled and gave a small, almost shy wave to

the cheering throng as she handed the horse's reins over to a very flustered but grateful driver.

'I don't know what spooked old Esmerelda,' he said, patting the horse's side, 'she's normally such a mild-mannered mare.' He put the battered top hat he was carrying back on and led the now-calm horse, with the undamaged carriage behind it, back up Sackville Street towards the Rotunda Hospital.

Molly shook her head and smiled over at Bram. *Yes*, thought Bram, smiling back at his friend, *Molly's back indeed!*

CHAPTER THREE:

GUESS WHO'S COMING TO BREAKFAST?

IN WHICH MOLLY DELIVERS KIPPERS AND BRAM FINDS OUT THAT
SMALL, ANGRY CHILDREN AREN'T EXACTLY A WALK IN THE PARK

Dawn was breaking as Bram and Molly returned to Bram's Buckingham Street house. From the carriage window Bram watched the pale sun rising, sending tendrils of cold light over the smoky Dublin rooftops, and sighed contentedly; his old friend Molly was back, and what night they had had!

After the incident with the runaway horse, and after the astonished crowd of onlookers had hugged Molly and clapped her back until it was sore and she had to ask them to stop, the Spooks had walked to Billy the Pan's home on the top floor of a ramshackle tenement building in Gloucester Street. Billy was the only one of The Sackville Street Spooks who actually had a family; all the others – Shep, Rose and even Molly herself – were orphans. As Bram climbed the rickety stairs, holding tight onto the broken banister and trying not to fall into gaping holes in the bare, carpetless steps, he thought how lucky he was to have *his* family. His mama and papa were gentle, reserved, quiet people who loved their son dearly (they told him so almost every day) and their home in Buckingham Street was spacious and warm, with fashionable flock wallpaper, comfy furniture to sit on, toasty beds to sleep in and a cosy fireplace in every room.

Billy's family home was much less grand than

Bram's; in fact it was the absolute *opposite* of grand. The wallpaper was definitely *not* made of fashionable flock; it was drab, dirty and torn, and where it did hang on the walls, it seemed to hang on with a kind of grim determination. Every piece of furniture seemed to be broken; all the seat cushions were burst open with rusty springs poking out, and the legs of the few tables and chairs in the small room bowed and twisted at ridiculous angles. The beds, if you could call them that, were just rough blankets lying on straw over bare floorboards. The home couldn't be described as spacious, it was only two tiny rooms; *How many people live here?* thought Bram. *Do they take turns to sleep?* There was only one fireplace, sooty and black, in which a few sticks and twigs sputtered with a desultory glow.

But what Billy's home lacked in size and opulence, it made up for in love. As soon as the Spooks reached the top landing of the tumbledown building a door was flung open and Billy's family, all of whom seemed to be wide awake, even at this late hour, piled out and dragged the five friends (and dog) inside with exclamations of delight. Molly was hugged and kissed, and Bram, who had never met most of Billy's family before, was surprised to find himself being hugged and kissed too, and equally surprised to find that he didn't mind being hugged and kissed by perfect strangers at all.

'How come they are all still awake?' he asked Molly in a whisper, 'It's almost one o'clock in the morning!'

Molly stretched her neck around to look at Bram from where she was being held in a tight bear-hug by one of Billy's many sisters. 'Billy's family are beggarmen, remember,' she whispered back, 'and beggarwomen too, of course — they have to work begging shifts during the night to keep the family in food and firewood. Begging is a full-time business, you know!'

Once they were all inside and all sitting down on the unsteady furniture around the puny fireplace, Billy's father, Georgie the Shovel, raised his wooden spade high in the air for silence. Like Billy with his saucepan hat, Georgie always had his shovel on his shoulder, its rounded blade shining with silver paint, to distinguish himself from all the other vagrants on the street. Every beggarman (or beggarwoman) needed their own way of standing out from the crowd of other vagabonds, and Georgie's massive silver shovel was his own particular gimmick. 'Molly Malone,' he boomed, 'welcome back to Dublin! Now – tell us all about your voyage over the ragin' foam of the Atlantic Ocean and all about your travels and adventures on the shores of Ameri-kay!'

Billy's mother appeared from the other room with a big tray filled with small slices of almost stale bread and butter, some of which had been sprinkled with small amounts of sugar, and one of Billy's sisters poured tea into chipped cups and jam jars from a kettle that had been heating on the tiny fire. As Bram sat listening to Molly's stories, he supped his tea and munched on the sugared bread. The bread was hard and chewy, but in the firelight with his friends around him, it tasted better than cake.

Molly told the group about the passage to New York, on a steam ship called *The Kunak*; it had taken two weeks, and poor Rose had been seasick every day.

'Molly!' cried Rose, slapping Molly's arm playfully, 'You didn't have to go an' tell them that!'

Molly giggled, 'It's true, though! She was always hangin' over the side of the ship pukin'! Rose spent so much time starin' down at the Atlantic Ocean that she was on first name terms with every fish between here and Newfoundland!'

Molly told them about New York with its tall buildings, brightly-lit shops and fine hotels – and its dangerous street gangs. 'There's a crowd called The Dead Rabbits,' she told them, 'Right cut-throats, they were. If you got on the wrong side of them, you'd be in real trouble – they put the Spooks in the ha'penny place! There was another gang called The Mangled Ferrets, but they weren't dangerous really; their trick was to stand on street corners playing music so bad that people would give them money to stop!'

She told them about the people they met, the friends they made, the strange and wonderful places they went, and the equally strange and wonderful food they ate. 'They have these little roundy bread rolls with a hole in the middle of them, like a hoop,' said Molly, 'and wait till you hear this: they boil them before they put them in the oven, and then they spread them with watery cheese paste and eat them!'

'And what kind of music do they have there? Apart from The Fangled Merits, of course,' asked Georgie the Shovel.

'All sorts,' laughed Molly, 'There are people in New York who come from all over the world – Italians, Greeks, Germans, Chinese – you hear all kinds of music, played on all sorts of weird instruments there. Every night is filled with music and dancin' and singin'!'

'Ah, I bet you missed the good aul' Irish airs while you were away,' said Georgie, putting down his shovel and picking up a battered accordion, 'C'mon kids, let's give Molly a grand aul' Irish welcome home.' With that, the children in the family produced a selection of old flutes, crooked tin whistles, partially-punctured pipes and slightly-broken bodhráns; one of the smaller boys even had a beat-up banjo to pluck; and they began to play and sing loudly and raucously.

'All beggarmen have a talent, Billy's family's talent is playing music,' said Molly to Bram as she hummed along delightedly. The music and dancing continued well into the early hours, and now and again there was a knock on the door, and they were joined by neighbours from the other rooms in the tenement. These neighbours, to Bram's surprise, weren't arriving to complain about the noise – they were coming to join in the fun!

Back on Buckingham Street, much later, the horse-drawn carriage came to a stop directly outside Bram's house. Bram looked up to the top of the three-storey red-brick building, the sun rising behind it. *My good gracious*, he thought, *if this were Billy the Pan's tenement, his entire family – all fourteen of them – would be living in only a quarter of the space of the top floor of mine.*

He stepped down from the carriage slowly, his legs weary from dancing and his throat sore from singing, and looked up at Molly. 'It's good to have you back, Mol,' he said to his friend, 'I'm sure I shall see you soon.'

'Not if I see you first!' said Molly, grinning at her pal, 'Only messin', I'm sure we'll both be together again, and much sooner than you think!' She rapped her knuckles on the ceiling of the carriage and the driver flicked the horse's reins. 'C'mon, Murphy,'

Molly shouted, 'off to the Imperial Hotel in Sackville Street; Rose will be there already and if we don't get a move on, she'll have stolen me hot water bottle!'

Bram stood at his gate, watching the carriage until it turned the corner onto Montgomery Street. He yawned a long YAAAAAWWWWNNNN, fished in his pocket for the door key, let himself in and quietly climbed the stairs to his bedroom. Once there, he changed into his pyjamas, picked up his diary and sighed happily as he got into his warm, comfortable bed. It wasn't quite up to Molly's Imperial Hotel standards, but all the same, Bram was very glad that *he* wasn't sleeping in a rough blanket on the cold floorboards like Billy probably was. *Billy's family have so little money*, he thought sleepily, *but so much of everything else.* He had every intention of writing about his amazing and unexpected night out in Dublin City in his journal, but as soon as his head hit the plump, soft pillow he was asleep, the diary open across his chest and the pencil falling soundlessly from his fingers onto the Chinese-patterned rug.

* * *

Bram was awakened by a soft knocking, not on the window this time, but on his bedroom door. He was confused, was it morning already? He seemed to have just laid his head down to sleep only seconds before. 'Excuse me,' said a muffled voice from the other side of the door, 'Master Bram, there's a visitor for you in the breakfast room.'

'Thanks, Lily,' he croaked to the maid, his voice still husky from the night before, 'I shall be down shortly.' As he washed in the porcelain basin on the mahogany stand in the corner of his room and got dressed, he wondered who the mysterious breakfast guest could be. He had made plenty of new friends at Reverend Woods' Academy, the new school his parents had enrolled him into after they had moved the family to Buckingham Street. He was popular at his school, in part because of his sporting ability – he was a strong cross-country runner and a star player on the rugby team – but also because of his wild imagination; he could keep his classmates, and some-times his tutors too, amused and enthralled for hours with his ingenious stories of decrepit mummies, creepy ghost-like apparitions, and evil Transylvanian counts. But as friendly as he was with his fellows in the Academy, none of them had yet come to call on him at home, not even on a Saturday. Looking in the mirror, he adjusted his collar and straightened his bow tie. *Well, I suppose I'd better see who has come to call*, he thought, *and just in time for breakfast too!*

Bram descended the stairs slowly, his legs still tired from the previous night's walking and dancing, and opened the door to the breakfast room. His eyes widened and, not for the first time in the last twenty-four hours, his mouth gaped open.

At the breakfast table – laid out by their housekeeper with the usual fresh white linen, sparkling silver cutlery and large bowls and dishes full of steaming sausages, bacon and scrambled eggs – sat his mama and his papa, and sitting between then, munching on a sausage was … MOLLY MALONE!

'Ah, Bram, my dear,' said his mother, putting down her knife and fork, 'your friend Miss Malone has come to visit! Do sit down and have a cup of tea.'

Bram sat down, his eyes wide and on Molly. 'Molly tells us she is of the Kildare Malones, isn't that right, Molly?' said Bram's mama, filling his bone-China teacup from a tall silver teapot.

'Yes, Ma'am,' said Molly, her pretend upper-class accent rich and slightly fruity. 'I am a ward of my Uncle, Bertram Florence-Malone. Uncle is a horse trainer with a large estate at the Curragh; we keep several hundred horses there.'

Bram lifted the teacup to his lips with a trembling hand – Molly's fake accent was high-pitched and nasal, almost a parody of plumminess; but Mama and Papa seemed to be taken in by it. At least, his mother did – his father was, as was usual, completely hidden behind by the newspaper he was reading.

'Molly was saying she met you at a rugby match when Reverend Woods' Academy played the Curragh Cavaliers.' Bram's mother's brow wrinkled, 'Funny, it's not a team I am familiar with … and you told her to call in the next time she found herself in the city. I'm so glad you did!'

'Bram,' continued his mother, 'dear Molly brought breakfast kippers! As well as owning huge tracts of land in Kildare, she tells us her family also have an interest in fishmongery, isn't that delightful?' Bram looked blankly at his mother, until he felt a sharp pain in his shin – Molly had kicked him under the table.

'Yes!' he squeaked, jerking his leg back from Molly's reach, 'most delightful, Mama!' He rubbed his shin and gave Molly a quizzical look. Molly winked at him and laughed a tinkling, elegant chuckle.

'Oh, Molly, dear!' exclaimed Mama, 'We had planned to visit the Museum of Natural History in the city this morning; it opened two years ago, and we simply haven't had the opportunity to visit yet – perhaps you would like to accompany us?'

'Is that the one with all the stuffed animals?' asked Molly in her wonky well-to-do accent. 'Why, I should be delighted to accompany you, my dear Mrs Stoker – that sounds like just the tickety-boo ticket; I do love animals!' She smiled sweetly across at Bram. Bram shook his head and had to smile back, which wasn't easy as he was currently biting his lips to stop himself from laughing. *Her fake accent is beyond ridiculous*, he thought, *how can it fool my mama and papa? It wouldn't fool a small child!*

'Papa,' said Mama, 'We should tell Carstairs to prepare the horse and to bring around the larger buggy.'

Papa, from behind his newspaper, harrumphed a HARRUMPHing noise. 'It's settled then, Molly shall come with us to the Museum! Perhaps you two young friends would like to wait in the drawing room while the carriage is made ready?'

Once in the drawing room, Bram let go of the giggles he had been suppressing.

'Wha'?' asked Molly, grinning at her pal, 'Was there somethin' wrong with my voice?'

Bram wiped his eyes, 'No, Mol, you sounded every inch like a properly prosperous young lady!'

Molly brushed down the front of her bottle-green silk dress and pushed a lock of curly red hair back behind her ear. Over the last few months she had got used to wearing fancy clothes – she and Rose had bought some fashionable dresses, gloves and hats while they were away in America, using the money from the 'very, very small' gemstones that had fallen out of the Crown Jewels – and now they both dressed like well-to-do young ladies, looking not at all like the street children they used to be (and still were at heart). But Molly thought she would never get used to the boots. She was so used to wearing shabby, worn-out, third-hand shoes, or no shoes at all. She often used to walk the Dublin streets bare-foot; most of The Sackville Street Spooks were used to the feeling of smooth cobblestones under their bare feet. Her new fancy boots were fine and com-fortable – they were tailor-made specially for her feet by a master shoemaker in New York – but, *holy moley*, there were so many buttons on them, it took *forever* to get them on and off!

She looked around the drawing room with its high ceilings, intricately-patterned wallpaper and white marble fireplace and thought that, although she had been in some grand hotels in New York City, she had never been in such an ornate room. She wasn't even too sure what a drawing room was, but she liked it. Her old home in Dublin had been a tumble-down shack at the side of the lock keeper's cottage at Newcomen Bridge on the Royal Canal; a draughty, dilapidated, wooden-walled ruin she shared with the rest of The Spooks. The ceiling there had been low – corrugated iron with holes through which the rain poured on wet days – and the walls weren't covered in gilt-framed paintings like this luxurious room, but

hung with racks of stolen silk handkerchiefs, pur-
loined handbags and an abundance of sundry other
ill-gotten gains. Her eyes fell on the tall oak bookcases standing opposite the drawing room window.
She ran to them and excitedly inspected the tightly
packed shelves, running her finger over the spines
of the multitude of books each shelf contained. 'So
many books, Bram!' she exclaimed, 'You must have
more books here than in Trinity College!'

'I hardly think so,' laughed Bram, 'Have you ever
been to the huge library in Trinity, the Long Room?
It's absolutely enormous! There are so many books
there, that if one laid them end-to-end, they should
reach all the way across the ocean to New York!'

Molly selected a book from the shelf and sat on
a dusky pink damask-covered sofa, looking closely
at the title on the book's spine. '*The Legend of Sleepy
Hollow* by Washington Irving,' she read. 'That Irving
fella's very popular in New York – do you mind if I
borrow this?' She slipped it into the voluminous car-
pet-bag she carried without waiting for an answer.

There was a soft knock on the door; it opened and
Lily the maid stuck her head around, 'Master Bram,

Miss; the buggy is waiting.'

Molly brushed down her dress again as Bram escorted her to the hall door. 'You know,' she whispered, glancing at Bram as they walked down the hallway, 'I don't think I've ever been called "Miss" in Dublin before – it's usually "Hey, you!" or "Get out of here!" they call me!'

Bram's mother talked incessantly on the carriage ride to Merrion Square, telling Molly interesting facts about every celebrated building and landmark they passed, and suggesting other notable places to visit while she was on her trip to Dublin. *This is gas*, thought Molly, *she really believes that I'm from Kildare and am just visiting the city – as if I wasn't born and bred in Dublin!* Bram's papa kept his eyes on his newspaper on the journey, and Bram was quiet too, content to look out the window – not that he could have gotten a word in edgeways with his mama's constant chattering, even if he tried.

The buggy pulled up at the north side of Merrion Square and Molly, Bram and Bram's parents alighted. 'Now,' said Mama as they walked towards the gate of the park at the centre of the Square, 'this is a private park, usually for the residents of Merrion Square exclusively, but Papa is employed at Dublin Castle, and the eminent gentlemen who work there enjoy the privilege of unfettered access to many parks throughout the city – isn't that quite the perk of the job? Papa is the Keeper of the Irish Crown Jewels at the Castle; did you know?'

As it happened, Molly *did* know. In fact, she was carrying the Irish Crown Jewels in the carpet bag she was holding; the *real* ones, not the fake ones made of glass, paste and gold-painted tin that Papa was guarding so diligently (and misguidedly) in the strong room of the Tavistock Tower in Dublin Castle! Molly coughed and blinked her eyes rapidly.

'Really?' she chirped innocently in her best la-di-dah young lady voice, 'How interesting!'

'I thought we might walk through the park on our way to the Museum,' said Bram's mother, 'and take a little of the lovely spring air.' Bram's father rolled up his newspaper and rolled his eyes too, but followed his wife towards the gate, motioning for the two children to tag along too.

The entrance to the park was overseen by a tall,

black-suited guard wearing a top hat; he smiled and swung the wrought-iron gate for their party as they approached. 'Mr Stoker,' he said, tipping the brim of his topper with a white-gloved hand. 'Nice to see you again, sir.'

The gardens were green and beautiful, with wide, well-kept lawns and flowerbeds blooming with spring colour. The tall trees that bordered the park were budding with new green leaves and they cast tall shadows across the grass as the spring sun rose higher in the clear morning sky. Here on there on the lawns were little groups of mothers and nannies with small children, sitting on immaculately clean picnic blankets laid neatly on the grass. The little girls were all dressed in frilly, colourful frocks, and most of the boys clad in what looked to Molly like tiny sailor uniforms, complete with striped collars and navy caps. The children were playing chasing, singing nursery rhymes and throwing India rubber balls to each other; all looked happy and carefree. All except one child – a tousled-haired miniature sailor with a screwed-up red face, who was screaming and stamping his feet on the grass of the manicured lawn

in a most alarming manner. His poor mother, wearing an extremely ornate powder-blue silk dress with
vast lace petticoats, looked on with an air of calm
resignation.

'Ahhh,' said Bram's mama, seemingly delighted,
'it's my old friend Lady Jane!' She crossed the grass
to her friend, with Bram, Molly and Bram's father
following in her wake. 'Miss Molly Malone,' she said,
'may I introduce my good friend Lady Jane Wilde!'
Lady Jane and Bram's mama air-kissed, 'And this is
Lady Jane's delightful son, Oscar.'

The small boy looked at both Bram and Molly
with a horrible-looking scowl on his face and
instantly made a decision to ignore them both completely. Molly thought the child was around four or
five years of age, but it was hard to tell when his face
was so contorted with fury. In fact, far from looking
like a little boy, Molly thought young Oscar bore a
much greater resemblance to a gargoyle from the
spires of St Patrick's Cathedral.

'AAAAARRRRGGGGGHHHHH!' the boy
bellowed, stamping his feet once again, 'MAMA!
How am I to colour my dragon if you have mis-

placed all two of my green crayons? To lose one green crayon may be regarded as misfortune; to lose both looks like carelessness!' He erupted again into frenzied screams, as his mother continued to pay him no attention.

Molly and Bram looked at one another, their eyebrows raised in amusement.

Bram's father shook his head and spoke for the first time, 'Bram, why don't you run along to the Museum with your friend, then we shall meet for elevenses afterwards? You know what your mother is like for talking.' He sighed quietly, his hands behind his back, 'We may be here for some time …'

Bram took another look at the ill-tempered terror, who by this stage had crumpled up his dragon picture and thrown it at his inattentive mother. He nodded gratefully to his papa, then the two friends trotted off across the grass.

They could still hear young Oscar Wilde's petulant howls as they crossed Merrion Street and walked through the gates of the Natural History Museum.

CHAPTER FOUR:

Let's Get Stuffed!

The Natural History Museum was a long, rectangular, white stone building attached to Leinster House, and Molly and Bram entered through a grand doorway at the top of Leinster Lawn. 'It only opened to the public a couple of years ago,' said Bram excitedly, 'The Royal Dublin Society had so many stuffed animals and rocks and things in its collection that it had to put up this building to exhibit them all!'

Just like the gate to Merrion Square Park, the door was opened for them by a tall, besuited man wearing a top hat. 'Good morning, young sir, young miss,' said the doorman cheerfully.

'Thank you, and a very good morning to you too!' replied Bram, with equal cheeriness.

Molly marvelled at how easy it was to gain entry to places when you were wearing the right clothes and speaking with the right accent. If she was wearing the clothes she used to wear – a faded blue dress, tattered petticoat, ragged shoes and torn stockings – and was speaking in her usual flat Dublin accent, she doubted that she, or any of the Sackville Street Spooks, would have even been allowed onto Leinster Lawn, let alone through the doors of this magnificent building. Far from greeting her like an old friend with a warm word and a welcoming wave, this doorman would have chased her away, with a great deal of shouting and shaking of his fists. She thought that Billy and Shep's current ragged clothes definitely wouldn't be welcome here!

Billy and Shep had elected to stay behind to look after the smallest member of the Spooks, Calico Tom, when Rose and Molly had announced that they were taking a trip to America. Billy had moved into their ramshackle shed at the side of the Royal Canal, and the three of them lived quite happily there for several weeks – until the police realised that Molly had decamped to New York and raided the shack in the middle of the night. Then the Peelers evicted the remaining Spooks and burned the tumbledown wooden cabin to the ground. But not before they carted off all the goodies inside. Billy had described in his letters to Molly how the Peelers had piled handcarts high with bundles of silk handkerchiefs, boxes of silver cutlery and bulging bags of fine leather pocketbooks. 'Dey tuk evvy-ting!' scrawled Billy in his handwritten (and atrociously spelled) letter from across the ocean, 'Dere is nuttin left of the shak except for burny stiks!'

Billy had to go back to live with his very large family at the top of the tenement in Gloucester Street, and their old friends, the fortune teller Madame Flo and her husband Wild Bert, had taken

Shep and Calico Tom in. Billy and Shep still met up for regular 'bobbing' sessions – pick-pocketing from the Quality on Sackville Street (old habits die hard) – but Calico Tom, at the ripe old age of seven, had retired from the swindling business and had gone to work with Madame Flo in her carnival sideshow tent. Being small for his age – even at seven years old he was no bigger than a toddler – he could fit comfortably under Madame Flo's fortune telling table, causing teacups to rattle and making her crystal ball 'magically' lurch and dance around to the amazement and bewilderment of her gullible punters. Flo and Bram treated Calico and Shep like the sons they never had, and Molly was mollified, as it were, that the two boys had somewhere safe and warm to live; somewhere they were loved … and welcome.

Molly and Bram strolled passed the doorman and through the small, dark foyer into the Museum. The main room was bright and airy, lit from high above by a huge glass ceiling, and they both blinked in the brightness as they took in their surroundings.

Molly gasped. Towering over them was a massive skeleton of some sort of gigantic deer, so tall that it its enormous antlers seemed to be scraping the glass of the Museum's ceiling. 'An elk!' exclaimed Bram, 'This is a giant deer, Mol; they used to be all over Ireland in the olden days.' Beyond the skeletal elk the main room stretched back into the distance, filled with cabinets with polished wooden bases, glass cases and glass-fronted shelves, all packed with exhibits. Above the main floor, which was covered in red and black diamond-shaped tiles, there was a mezzanine level of wooden-floored walkways with iron guard-rails around all four sides of the room; each of these balconies were lined with glass cases. And above this mezzanine level was *another* mezzanine level, with its own set of packed display cases too. The sides of the top balcony were decorated with rows of deer, ante-lope, goat, bison, zebra and moose heads. All were staring down with slightly blank expressions, making Molly feel like she was being watched.

'My goodness gracious,' said Bram, 'there is so much to look at here that I am very sorry we didn't think to bring a packed lunch!'

They strolled through the room examining the displays as they walked. There were cases of stuffed

Irish birds, displayed perching on branches decorated with green silk leaves or on grey-painted *papier-mâché* rocks; from small birds like the finch to larger ones like the barnacle goose, each was represented in a life-like pose.

Molly's favourite was the puffin. 'Ah, look at this one,' she said to Bram, 'its beak is all the colours of the rainbow!'

There were display cases containing Irish mammals, with stoats, pine martens, ferrets and hares, all depicted gambolling on fake grass or horse-playing on leaves made out of painted paper. There were even displays of stuffed rats and mice, and although Molly wasn't fond of either animal – she had seen enough of both rats *and* mice in her days living in the shack beside the Royal Canal – she was happy to stand beside Bram as he stared at them with such interest and glee.

The Museum was quiet, and the air inside had a slightly musty smell, which Molly imagined may have come from the multitude of stuffed animals it held. A little weary from all the excitement of the night before, she sat on the side of a tall display case and watched Bram as he scurried from one display case to another, examining the animals within and carefully reading the handwritten information card on each. *He's like a bee*, she thought, *buzzin' around from flower to flower collecting pollen!*

Bram wandered over and read the information card on the case Molly sat on, then looked at the contents of the case. 'You might want to move, Mol,' he said, 'I have a feeling someone might fancy you for a spot of light lunch!'

Molly looked behind her and almost jumped in fright. Inside the glass case was the biggest, angriest-looking bear that Molly had ever seen. It was covered in brown fur and was standing to its full height, its two front paws raised as if about to attack. Each paw was tipped with long, gleaming claws, each as sharp and as deadly as a dagger. The bear's mouth was open wide, showing two rows of vampire-like fangs, and it seemed to be roaring out a loud, angry warning.

At the huge bear's feet was a tiny version of itself; this smaller bear didn't look angry, though – it was sitting, and seemed to be happily playing with a pinecone.

'That's a grizzly!' said Molly, 'I've seen them in New York, when we were up in the woods.' Bram looked astonished, 'You mean you've actually seen these in real life?' Molly nodded. 'Yup. That's a mammy one,' she said, pointing at the huge beast, 'She's not really on the attack here, she's just warning us off to protect her little cub.' Molly looked down at the smaller bear, 'She just doesn't want any harm to come to her baby.'

Suddenly there was a commotion from the doorway of the library and a large group of schoolchildren trooped in. All were wearing short grey trousers and navy jackets with school crests. Leading them was a lady dressed in black with an enormous bun of jet-black hair at the top of her head. She wore small *pince-nez* spectacles on the bridge of her long, hooked nose, and fluttered about her charges flapping her arms like the wings of a giant crow.

'Mrs Harker!' muttered Bram, his voice a whisper, 'Good golly, Molly! It's the headmistress from my old boarding school! We must hide!' Molly looked confused. 'Hide? Why? I'm not hidin' – I'll get me new dress all dirty and I'd have to go around for the rest of the day lookin' like an eejit!' Bram grabbed her arm and pulled her behind a glass case, realised it was made of glass and therefore see-through, and pulled her behind a pillar instead. 'It's just that I never actually formally left Mrs Harker's Academy, I sort of just ran away from it. I think she may not be, shall we say, overly happy to see me!'

Molly rolled her eyes and smiled at her friend. She could well understand how he may have wanted to run away from school – she had never been to school herself, unless you counted the lessons she had been made attend in the Workhouse she had been imprisoned in when she was younger.

From their viewpoint behind the pillar they could see the school group ascending the stairs to the balcony level above. Bram pulled Molly further behind the pillar, into an alcove with a big, shuttered window. Sitting on the red and black tiled floor under the white window shutters was a boy with black hair. He wore grey shorts like the boys from Bram's old school, but Bram didn't think he was a pupil there: he wasn't wearing the same school blazer – this chap's jacket was green, not navy. The boy's knees were drawn up and resting on them was big sketchbook. Pencil in hand, he looked up at Bram and Molly with huge brown eyes, then immediately looked down again and continued sketching. 'What are you drawin'?' asked Molly, craning her neck too see the sketchpad. 'Give us a look.' The boy's head lowered, and he sketched even harder than before. Molly looked into the glass case at the side of the alcove. 'Are you drawin' these seashells?' she asked, squinting at the information card in the case, 'What are they called – naughty-less?'

'Nautilus shells,' whispered Bram. 'C'mon, Mol, Mrs Harker's gang have all gone upstairs, we'll make a break for it.' He looked at the boy on the floor; he had barely raised his head. 'I don't think this young fellow here wants to be friendly, anyway.'

It was Molly's turn to pull Bram back by the arm this time. 'Bram,' she said, their backs turned to the young artist on the floor, 'maybe this lad *wants* to be friendly but is, you know, too *shy* to speak to us.' Molly raised her ginger eyebrows, 'Madame Flo always said that the greatest kindness you can show to a shy person is just to be friendly to them; to give them a bit of your time. And she should know – she's the One Who Knows All, the Fortune Teller's Fortune Teller, the White Witch of –'

'–Westmoreland Street,' said Bram, 'Yes, I know …' He walked back to the boy and, giving Molly a wink, hunkered down beside him to have a closer look at his sketchpad. 'I say!' he exclaimed. 'Those nautilus shells you've drawn are really good – you're very talented!' The boy looked up at Bram and gave a very small, very shy smile. Bram took this as an encouraging sign and continued, 'This is an astonishing place, isn't it? Are you here with a school group?' The boy shook his head. 'Oh,' said Bram, 'are you visiting with your folks, then?' The small boy shook his black-haired head, opened his mouth to speak, and then abruptly closed it again.

'Well, how have you gotten here, then?' asked Molly, 'You didn't come by yourself, and you hardly live here in the Museum.'

'I *do* live here,' said the boy in a small voice, 'I live here with my uncle. He is a professor of Animal Biology, visiting from Bombay in India and I have been sent to stay with him while he's working at the Museum.' Once the boy started speaking, there seemed to be no stopping him; his speech flowed like water gushing from a burst dam. 'My name is Sanjit, Sanjit Chandra, and my mother sent me to my uncle in Dublin because it is too dangerous for me at home in India; there is a rebellion there against British rule and there is a lot of fighting. At night-time there is shouting and sometimes loud bangs. I don't like loud bangs, so mother sent me to stay here – I am living with my mother's brother, my Uncle Seth. I had never met him before I came here. Well, I did when I was a baby of course, but I don't remember him. My mother told me he has a big beard, just like my grandfather, so I recognised him straight away. We have rooms in the basement of the Museum, but I prefer to stay up here where it is bright and quiet. I like to be by myself and to draw.'

'You must know the Museum very well,' said Molly, 'It's our first time here; could you give us a tour?'

Sanjit hopped to his feet, a shy smile on his face, delighted to be asked. In fact, he was delighted to be spoken to at all; most children his age seemed to prefer to ignore him. Even at home in Bombay he often found himself sitting alone on the veranda of his family home, shielding his eyes from the sun as other children played in the dusty street. A few may have glanced over towards him while they played, but none ever called to him to join in. 'That would be my pleasure!' he said, and with his smile growing bigger with every step, led them on a tour of the Museum, stopping at every display case and speaking at length, and with great authority, about the animal within. Molly was entranced as she walked along listening with interest to Sanjit as he told them all about the migration patterns of Canada geese and the hibernation habits of the common dormouse.

Bram, impressed as he was with the boy's depth of animal knowledge, was only half-listening. He was distracted, listening to Sanjit with one ear and keeping the other pricked for any sound of Mrs Harker's school group on the upper mezzanine level; every footstep he heard on the wooden balcony above made his heart jump, and a couple of times Molly turned around only to find Bram hiding behind a pillar, looking upwards nervously.

Sanjit brought them over to the case Molly and

Bram had looked at before, in which the two stuffed grizzly bears, one huge and one tiny, were standing. The bears were flanked by other stuffed animals, all of which looked like they had seen better days. There was a yellow mountain lion with a missing ear, a big grey wolf who was missing half its tail, as well as a small brown moose with a missing antler and an ancient crocodile. The green stuffed crocodile was standing on its wrinkly rear legs and looked like it was waving at them with the one front claw it had left. Stuffing was sticking out through a split seam in its leathery tail. 'I'm sure crocodiles don't stand up like that,' said Bram, 'I thought they just scuttled along the ground like big lizards.'

'They do!' exclaimed Sanjit, 'But this crocodile is no ordinary crocodile; this animal belonged to a pirate!' He sat down on the side of the case, directly under the huge grizzly bear, 'All these stuffed animals — the wolf, the bears, the mountain lion, the crocodile, even the moose — were once part of a pirate crew.' Molly and Bram, their curiosity aroused, sat on the ground to listen.

'A hundred years ago, there was an Irish pirate

called Captain Luke Lamprey,' said Sanjit, 'He was born in Dublin and ran away to sea when he was very young. He became a sailor to start with, but the captain of the ship he served on was very cruel. Luke Lamprey led the crew in a mutiny against him and took the ship. They made the captain walk the plank like pirates used to force their enemies to do. When they heard about the mutiny, the authorities started calling Lamprey a pirate, so he decided if he is being *called* a pirate, he may as well *be* one.'

Sanjit took a long, deep breath and continued, 'Captain Lamprey turned out to be a very good pirate – he sailed to the Indian Ocean, robbed lots of ships and stole lots of gold – but his problem was he didn't really get on with other people; his crew were always quitting their jobs and leaving his ship.' Sanjit motioned back toward the display case with his thumb, 'So he recruited his own crew, a crew that would not quit. A crew of stuffed animals that he stood on the deck to make it look like he had a full company of cutthroats on board! The wolf was manning the cannons, the crocodile was clasping a cutlass and the moose was armed with a musket. When other ships saw *The Menagerie* – that was what Captain Lamprey called his pirate ship – they looked at all the wild animals on board, were terrified and ran away.' Sanjit blinked, 'I mean, of course, they sailed away, or swam away if Captain Lamprey had sunk their ship.'

'So, how did Captain Lamprey's crew come to be in the Natural History Museum?' asked Bram.

'Ahh,' said Sanjit, raising his eyebrows, 'that's quite the story ...' Sanjit hadn't spoken this many words in a long time, and now he had started storytelling he found that he liked it.

'You see, Captain Lamprey was infamous in the Indian Ocean, where he had seized and looted many ships. But one day he picked on the wrong boat; a treasure ship that belonged to the Sultan of Rajapur, the richest man in all of India. The ship was painted gold, with tall white sails, and was said to carry the most precious gemstone in all of India: the Rajapur Ruby. This ruby was said to be the size of a big apple or a cannonball! It was heart-shaped and glowed red with an unearthly inner light. They said that ladies of the sultan's court who laid eyes upon the magnificent jewel fainted on the spot and had to be revived by the Sultan's doctors with smelling salts. The ruby was the Sultan's pride and joy.'

'So,' said Sanjit, his big brown eyes wide, 'when the Sultan found out his treasure ship was captured and his precious Rajapur Ruby was stolen, he engaged the services of the Royal British Navy and privateers working for the British East India Company to get it back! *The Menagerie* was pursued by many navy frigates, who chased it for months and months, across the Arabian Sea, over the Indian Ocean, around the Cape of Good Hope, and all the way to the Irish Sea.'

Molly and Bram sat while Sanjit spoke, enthralled with the story. 'Eventually,' said Sanjit, 'Lamprey and his skeleton crew made land here in Dublin, sailing *The Menagerie* as far as they could up into the marshes at Mud Island.'

'Mud Island!' cried Molly, 'I know that place well! That's where my shack is, or rather, was! It used to be a well-known area for smugglers, and there are loads of local legends about pirates and the like!'

'The local people took in Captain Lamprey and his crew and gave them shelter, then the Captain sank his own ship, *The Menagerie*, to hide it from the British – he scuttled it, and it disappeared down into the muddy marshes – but not before he unloaded these animals,' Sanjit gestured towards the stuffed animals in the cases behind, 'as well as all the treasure, of course. With the help of the Mud Island folk he smuggled the animals away into the care of an old acquaintance of his from the Royal Dublin Society, a Doctor Bartholomew Cobb – that's how they ended up here in the Museum.'

'But,' continued Sanjit, 'Nobody knows what became of Captain Lamprey himself, nor the Rajapur Ruby – they both disappeared and neither were ever seen again! The British Navy returned to the Sultan empty-handed.' Sanjit smiled and sat back.

Molly and Bram looked at each other. 'What a story!' said Bram, 'How do you know so much about a pirate from Dublin?'

Sanjit smiled a shy smile, 'It's a well-known story in Bombay – the tale of how the Rajapur Ruby was stolen; every child knows it there. As well as that, I read all about Captain Lamprey in the Library at Trinity College. My uncle has access to the Long

Library through his work at the Museum, and he allows me to–'

'SANJIT!' said a sudden loud, booming voice that startled all the three children, 'What have I told you about talking to strangers?' A tall man stood over them, glaring at them with fiery brown eyes beneath jet black, bristling eyebrows. He had a long, black, pointed beard and his shiny moustache curled at either end like the coiled tips of a lashing whip. He wore a crisp navy suit, the trouser creases as sharp as dagger blades, along with a dazzling white shirt. He may have been wearing a dickie-bow, a bootlace tie or even a cravat, but if he was, Bram thought he'd never know which – the man's waist-length beard was too long to see either way. A long brown cigar was clenched between the man's gleaming white teeth, its smoking tip glowing ruby red.

'Uncle Seth,' stammered Sanjit, 'these – these people aren't strangers … they are …'

'Miss Molly Malone, at your service,' said Molly chirpily, sticking out her hand for the tall man to shake, 'and this is Master Bram Stoker – we are friends of Sanjit.'

Uncle Seth ignored her proffered hand and continued glaring at his nephew. He seemed to be growling as he breathed.

'Emmm,' said Bram, looking from Uncle Seth to Sanjit and then back again. 'Look at the time, we'd better be off for elevenses!'

'Elevenses? Your father said something about that earlier; what are elevenses?' whispered Molly, her eyes on Uncle Seth.

'You know, Mol,' said Bram, 'coffee and a snack between breakfast and lunch – elevenses.'

'Shouldn't that be called *brunch,* you know, like the words *breakfast* and *lunch* combined? That makes a lot more sense than *elevenses* – *elevenses* just sounds silly!' said Molly. She was surprised that anyone should want another meal between breakfast and lunch, and that it was apparently so customary a meal amongst the Quality that they actually felt that they had to give it a name of its own, especially one as ridiculous as *elevenses*.

Bram *a-hemmed* a quiet *a-hem,*. 'Not the time to be making up words, Mol.'

With a haughty glare at Molly and Bram, Uncle

Seth folded over his long frame and grabbed Seth's short arm roughly with his lengthy one. 'Come with me, boy,' he growled around the cigar he held clamped between his teeth, 'You don't need friends.'

'I say, sir,' said Bram, '*do* be gentle with that chap!' As Uncle Seth began to tug his small nephew away, Molly came close and quickly whispered in the boy's ear, 'Everybody needs friends, Sanjit – meet us at the main door tomorrow morning, 10 o'clock …' The huge man and the tiny boy disappeared through a door marked STAFF ONLY. The door slammed behind them, leaving Bram and Molly standing in the quiet of the Museum, breathing in the pungent fumes left by Uncle Seth's rancid cigar.

'I suppose,' said Bram with a cough, when the smoke had cleared, 'we actually had better go and meet Mama and Papa for elevenses.' Molly shook her head, 'You mean *brunch* – I told you already, elevenses is such a silly word for a snack; my word "brunch" is much better. And while I'm at it, The Natural History Museum is a bit of a mouthful to say. It's full of stuffed animals – there's enough here to fill Dublin Zoological Gardens – I think a better, snappier name for the Museum would be … The Dead Zoo!'

'The Dead Zoo?' said Bram as they walked past the doorman and out into the fresh March air, 'No – that's a terrible name; it will never catch on.'

They walked across the lawn and back towards the park, neither knowing that from a ground floor window in the Museum, Sanjit's Uncle Seth was watching them with glowering dark eyes, his face shrouded by cigar smoke.

The Diary of Master Abraham Stoker
Saturday 19th of March, 1859
19 Buckingham Street, Dublin

Dearest Diary,
Well, what an amazing thirty-six hours the last thirty-six hours have been!

First of all, I got my dearest wish when Molly Malone unexpectedly turned up at my window and whisked me off for a night on the town! Oh Diary, I was carousing with my friends The Sackville Street Spooks once again! We halted the gallop of a runaway horse (oh, very well, Molly did!) and we danced and

sang and gadded about with beggars and vagabonds until the early hours – I have to admit I was in absolute heaven!

After that I had barely put my weary head down to sleep when we were off again; this time to 'The Dead Zoo', where we made a new friend – albeit one with an uncle who doesn't seem all that keen on Molly and myself ...

And finally, dear Diary, the entire gang is to meet tomorrow to go to something that Molly refers to as the 'Waxies' Dargle', and we are bringing our new pal Sanjit along with us.

Dear Diary, I have no idea what a 'Waxie' is, let alone what the definition of a 'Dargle' might be; but when it comes to entertainment, excitement and adventure, I put my trust in my dearest friend, Molly. Well ... I mean my dearest friend that isn't a diary!

Until tomorrow, dearest Diary,

Bram

PABLO FANQUE'S CIRCUS ROYAL
AT RINGSEND GREEN, DUBLIN

FOR ONE AFTERNOON ONLY
BEING THE OCCASION OF THE MUCH CELEBRATED
WAXIES' DARGLE
A GRAND DAY OUT IN WHICH MR FANQUE ESQ. PROMISES A SURFEIT OF DELICIOUS PICNIC DELICACIES AND NOTEWORTHY CARNIVAL NOVELTIES
ON SUNDAY AFTERNOON, MARCH 20TH, 1859.

Messrs. FANQUES, KITE & HENDERSON, having been some days in preparation, assure the Public that their production will be second-to-none. A splendid time is guaranteed for all!

Mr. WILD BERT FLORENCE will introduce his
CELEBRATED HORSE
BUTTERCUP
Well known to be the horse of foremost intelligence
IN THE WORLD

Mr. HENDERSON will, for the first time in Dublin, introduce his Astonishing
TRAMPOLINE LEAPS
AND SOMERSETS
Over Man & Horses, through Hoops & over Garters, and lastly, through a Hogshead of REAL FIRE!
IN THESE PURSUITS MR. H. CHALLENGES ALL COMPETITION!

GOD SAVE THE QUEEN!

HENNESSEY & WEBB, PRINTERS AND BOOKSELLERS, GREYSTONES

CHAPTER FIVE:

THE WAXIES' DARGLE

IN WHICH THE SPOOKS VISIT THE WAXIES' DARGLE, AND MOLLY SHOWS OFF HER ARCHERY EXPERTISE

Bram was waiting in the morning sunshine at the hall door of his house at Buckingham Street when the horse-drawn buggy pulled up at the gate. Inside the open-topped carriage sat Molly and Shep, with Rose sitting across from them holding Her Majesty. The brown dog barked excitedly when she saw Bram, putting her paws on the side of the carriage and giving him a doggy smile with her pink tongue lolling out.

'Good morning, girl,' Bram said to the mutt, giving her furry head a ruffle. 'Where's Billy the Pan?'

'Right here, sir!' said Billy from the driver's seat, tipping the brim of the top hat he was wearing instead of his customary battered saucepan, 'And where shall sir be going on this fine morning?'

Bram laughed as Molly reached down to help him up into the carriage. 'Billy's our driver today,' explained Molly, 'We had to – ahem – *borrow* this cab for the trip this morning. We're not made of money, and the cash I got from the couple of little diamonds that fell out of the Crown Jewels won't last forever. That hotel that me an' Rose are stayin' in costs a pretty penny too. But don't worry, we'll give the cab back when we're finished. The horse's name is Betty, by the way!'

'Speaking of diamonds,' said Bram, 'Where's the carpet bag you had with the jewels inside? We have to put those back sooner or later you know, Mol.'

'Don't worry about that either,' said Molly, 'The bag is somewhere safe. And we *will* get the Jewels back to Dublin Castle. Sooner or later ...' She winked at Bram and called out to the young carriage driver, his top hat a bit too big for his head and falling down over his eyes, 'Whip-crack-away, Billy! We are off to the Waxies' Dargle!' Billy hooshed up his topper, gave Betty a light tap on the backside with the whip, and the buggy moved off.

As the carriage rolled down Montgomery Street and towards Carlisle Bridge where they would cross the River Liffey, curiosity got the better of Bram. 'Okay, Mol,' he said, 'you have to tell me – what's a Waxies' Dargle?'

'The waxies,' explained Molly, as Rose and Shep looked at each other and rolled their eyes, 'are cobblers – people who make shoes. They are called "waxies" because they coat the threads they use to sew shoes together with wax to make them waterproof.'

'And what's a Dargle, then?' asked Bram.

'*The* Dargle is a river in Bray – that's a small town way down south, outside Dublin,' said Molly, 'The waxies used to organise a trip for city folk a couple o' times a year to go to the Dargle river in Bray and have a big picnic on the banks.' Bram looked slightly anxious, 'We're not going all the way to Bray today, are we?' To Bram, Bray seemed to be *miles* away!

'No, you eejit!' laughed Rose, holding tight on to Her Majesty who was trying to jump out of the carriage to chase a pigeon she spotted in the gutter at the side of Sackville Street, 'We are only goin' to Ringsend!'

'The thing about city folk is they don't really like to be outside of the city – the trip all the way out to Bray was a bit too much of a trip for them!' said Molly. Bram could sympathise with this point of view – if they were going to try to go to Bray this morning, it'd probably be dark before they got there! 'So,' continued Molly, 'they came to a compromise with the waxies, and had their picnic on the big green between Irishtown and Ringsend instead. They still call it the Waxies' Dargle, though.'

'And it's more of a funfair now than a picnic, isn't it, Mol?' said Shep, 'They have slides an' swingin' boats an' merry-go-rounds an' chair-o-planes an' all sorts there!'

'Yup,' said Molly, 'And that's not all – today they

have a circus!' She unfolded a long paper poster and handed it to Bram. At the top it had a picture of a team of trapeze artists balancing on each other in what Bram guessed was a sort of ungainly human pyramid; the poor man at the bottom-most of which was tottering about on a wooden skittle. Beside that was an illustration of a man leaping over a white horse. 'PABLO FANQUE'S Circus Royal' it said at the top, 'At Ringsend Green for ONE Afternoon Only!' Bram read through the poster with its promised clowns, acrobats, tightrope walkers and amazing feats of astounding strength, until something towards the end of the sheet caught his eye.

'Wild Bert Florence will Introduce his Celebrated Horse Buttercup,' read Bram, delight in his voice, 'Well Known to be the Horse of Foremost Intelligence in the World – Molly, is Wild Bert going to be here today?'

'Of course!' replied Molly, 'And his good lady wife Madame Flo too!'

Just then Billy pulled back on the horse's reins and the buggy came to a stop outside the gates of Natural History Museum. Molly leant out of the carriage and, putting her two smallest fingers into her mouth, gave an ear-splitting trio of whistled notes – two high and one low – so loud that poor Betty the horse got a fright and reared up slightly.

A small face appeared nervously around the side of the building and gave a timid wave. 'Molly!' exclaimed Shep, jumping down from the carriage, 'You didn't tell me that your new friend was the same as me!' Shep ran towards the shy boy and embraced him warmly. Sanjit looked shocked at first to be hugged by a stranger, but then he smiled broadly and returned the hug, and the two boys walked hand in hand back to the buggy. 'You see, Sanjit,' said Molly, beaming, 'I knew we'd all be best pals straight away!' Shep sat with his arm still around Sanjit, 'More than that, Mol, we are like brudders!'

* * *

The green at Ringsend was so packed with people that Bram couldn't see the green part at all – the only green things he could see were the trees around the edges and a couple of green coats and jackets in the crowd. Here and there were gaps in the crowd, like clearings in a forest, where picnic blankets were laid on the ground; but unlike the clean, pristine ones Bram had seen in Merrion Square, these ones were tatty, torn and slightly mucky from the many grimy children who clambered upon them, eating sloppy sandwiches and playing with muddy balls and broken, one-eyed dolls.

A massive man emerged from the throng of people and ambled towards the children as they clambered down from the carriage. His head was shaved, his nose was bent out of shape and his arms were so brawny they looked like they were going to burst out of the sleeves of the grey jacket he was wearing. Sanjit cowered back, but the rest of the Spooks smiled and waved in greeting.

'Hiya, Molly!' said the huge man in an unexpectedly high, flute-like voice, 'It's great to have ya back!' Molly stuck her small hand out and shook his gigantic one, 'It's great to *be* back, Cornelius!'

'Cornelius is a carnival strongman,' Molly said to Sanjit as they made their way through the crowd, 'he's a champion bare-knuckle boxer too!'

'But don't worry about him, he's as gentle as a kitten,' added Bram, 'and has a surprisingly lovely singing voice to boot!'

As well as picnicking families, there were people selling fruit from net bags on their backs, sandwiches of cheese and bacon from trays, and warm sausages from covered wicker baskets. Fishmongers were selling their wares of cockles and mussels, calling out that the unfortunate shellfish were 'Alive, alive oh!' Bram had already had his breakfast, but he still couldn't keep his mouth from watering slightly, not at the thought of the fishy-smelling cockles and mussels, but at the idea of biting into a lovely, big, juicy sausage sandwich. He looked down at Her Majesty and saw that her tongue was hanging out almost as much as his was at the smell of all the delicious food!

A few people in the crowd recognised Molly as she passed by, and there were many 'Howr'ya, Mollys' and 'You're lookin' well, Mollys' to be heard, as well as lots of people thanking her for various favours she had done for them (or their mother, or their auntie) in the past. One woman shook Molly by the hand and thanked her enthusiastically for stealing a fresh turkey for her husband's birthday dinner, while another man praised her for pinching the exact satin dress his wife had been gazing at in the window of Clery's department store for the last two years. Some of the crowd even took to singing the song that was becoming popular amongst the Dublin fishmongers.

'In Dublin's fair city,' they sang, 'Where the girls are so pretty, I first set my eyes on sweet Mol–'

'That's enough!' cried Molly, cutting them off, but Bram thought she looked secretly delighted with her unasked-for fame, and he himself was proud of his fairly famous friend.

'Bram,' said Sanjit quietly, 'those people were thanking Molly for *stealing* things for them; is Molly a thief?'

Bram laughed. 'She's not just a thief, Sanjit,' he said, 'she's the best sneak thief in Dublin and the most cunning pickpocket ever to, well, ever to pick a pocket!' Sanjit's eyes widened. 'But don't worry,' said Bram, 'Molly and her gang of Spooks don't steal because they're bad people; they just steal because they're hungry.' Bram looked at his group of pals, as they walked through the crowd shaking hands and getting claps on the back from grateful people. 'Apart from Billy the Pan, The Sackville Street Spooks are all orphans, and if you are unlucky enough to be an orphan in Dublin you only seem to have two choices – you either go to the Workhouse or you live on the streets and fend for yourself. Molly and the gang prefer not to go to the Workhouse, so they steal for a living instead.'

Sanjit looked up at his new friend and nodded. 'It is the same in Bombay,' he said, 'some children have parents and houses and are happy like me, and some have to steal or beg. Even some holy men in India go from town to town and village to village begging for food – they think it is a sin to have possessions or money!'

At the far end of the green was a row of small, brightly coloured tents with various signs, strange contraptions and brightly painted targets set up in front of them, and behind that was the biggest tent Bram had ever seen. It was the height of a house – nearly as tall as Bram's three-storey home in Buckingham Street – with its lofty walls made of red and white candy-striped canvas. Its roof was surrounded

by a scalloped fringe that arched upwards in a swoop-
ing curve to the apex, where a huge flag flew. The
flag was fluttering in the breeze that came in from
Dublin Bay and as the group of friends reached the
crescent of sideshow tents, Bram could read three
words painted in red and gold on the fluttering flag:
FANQUE'S CIRCUS ROYAL.

Suddenly Molly and Bram found themselves
enveloped in two strong arms. 'Well, gosh howdy!'
cried a loud, American-accented voice, 'If it ain't
my two favourite, I say *favourite*, chick-a-dees!' The
voice – and indeed the arms – belonged to a tall man
wearing a snow-white suit. The suit's jacket lapels
were encrusted in shiny blue rhinestones, and there
was a row of the same topaz-coloured glass gems
down the outside of each white trouser leg. He wore
white leather cowboy boots with silver spurs, and a
wide-brimmed white cowboy hat with a long blue
feather in the brim. His elaborately curled moustache was grey, as was his neat goatee beard. His eyes
were ice-blue and sparkling with pleasure.

'Wild Bert!' shouted Bram, delighted to see his old
friend.

'In person, lil' gentleman!' said Bert, smiling broadly and showing a row of gleaming white teeth, one of which was glittering silver, 'Now, I hear you guys would like to go the circus – is that right?' The children nodded enthusiastically. 'Can I get a YAA-HOOO?' said Bert.

'YAA-HOOO!' cried the children, almost as one. 'Can I get a YEEEEEE-HAAAAAAAAWW-WWW?' said Bert, laughing.

'YEEEEEE-HAAAAAAAAWWWWW!!' cried the children, Sanjit and Shep pumping their fists into the air.

'An' who's this new little guy here?' asked Bert, his well-manicured hand on Sanjit's shoulder.

'That's our new friend, Sanjit,' said Molly, 'he's come here from India!'

Wild Bert smiled, 'India, huh? Well, welcome friend; I'm from a land far-a-ways too – but I hope you'll feel as home here in Dublin as I do!'

Wild Bert handed each of them a numbered ticket, 'Here you go, good buddies – ringside seats for each and every one of you, I even got one for Her Majesty here!' He petted the smiling dog and then raised

his massive cowboy hat, '*Adieu,* as they say in Gay
Par-ee; I gotta go get my hosses an' animals ready
for the show – they do so love performin' for all the
children. They were born into the life; bred for it you
might say, just like me! The show starts in twenny
minutes – why don't you guys go visit some of the
sideshow attractions while you wait? I'm pretty cer-
tain that Madame Flo is hangin' around here someplace!' With that, he whipped off his white hat with
a flourish and gave them a low, theatrical bow. Wild
Bert then strutted back towards the Big Top, handing out paper flyers advertising *Pablo Fanque's Circus
Royal* to would-be patrons as he went.

'Molly,' said Bram, 'It's great to see Bert, but I have
one question: what's a "hoss"?' Molly laughed and
dragged him towards the sideshow carnival tents.

They found Madame Flo standing with her
arms folded in front of her small, multicoloured
tent, watching customers take turns at the Test-
Your-Strength machine. The machine was painted
blue and yellow and consisted of a tall, rectangular
wooden column with a painted scale that went from
ONE at the bottom to TEN at the top. There was a

red arrow attached to the pillar, a brass bell at the top and a wooden dome at the base. When the queueing punters got their turn, they had to hit the dome with a large wooden mallet as hard as they could and send the arrow up the scale. The harder they hit the dome with the mallet, the further the arrow would travel upwards. Strong, muscular guys like Cornelius could send the arrow right the way up to number TEN, ring the bell at the top and win a prize – in fact, poor Cornelius had got the arrow to TEN and won the top prize (two shillings and a bacon sandwich) so many times that the owner had barred him from playing – but most regular customers could only manage to get it as far as FIVE or SIX.

Madame Flo's face brightened when she saw the Spooks, and she quickly called Calico Tom to come out of the tent to say hello. Calico was delighted to see Bram again and hugged him around the knee, which, being so small, was as far up Bram as he could reach. Madam Flo too, hugged each of the Spooks in turn. Although he had never met her before, Sanjit hugged Flo back extra tightly. She was dressed in a long, flowing purple dress with wide orange cuffs on the sleeves, and every one of her fingers was adorned with a gold or silver ring with a coloured gem. On her head she wore a large navy-blue velvet turban topped with a long, orange ostrich feather.

'I'm so sorry, Ma'am,' stuttered Sanjit through a huge smile, 'but you look so much like my lovely Aunties back at home – I could almost be in Bombay!'

'This is Sanjit,' said Molly, gesturing to the small boy, who was smiling nervously up at Flo as he hugged her, 'Sanjit, this is my old pal, Calico Tom, and the lady you're hugging is the Amazing and Uncanny Madame Florence – the Seer of the What-Is-To-Come, the One Who Knows All, the Seventh Daughter of a Seventh Daughter, the White Witch of Westmoreland Street; with her crystal ball she can behold events that are yet to happen and with the power of her mind she can spy far into the future.' Sanjit waved shyly at Calico Tom and then hugged the fortune teller again.

Flo laughed a tinkling laugh and rubbed his head, 'How are all of yiz, kiddos?' She put her hand to her turban and closed her eyes dramatically, 'I can see a lot of fun yet to come, for all of you!'

Sanjit finally let go of his hug. 'You mean you can see into our future?' he asked, his eyes wide.

'No, love,' said Flo, 'I can see tickets for the circus yiz have in your hands!'

'MOLLY MALONE!' shouted a voice from behind them. The Spooks turned to see a bushy-haired girl in a ragged dress and grimy pinafore pushing her way towards them through the crowd. A small knee-high dog with rat-coloured fur followed behind her.

'Well, well, well,' said Molly, crossing her arms, 'Hetty Hardwicke – I thought I might meet you here.' The rest of the Spooks stood beside Molly, to show a united front to her rival. Her Majesty glared a doggy glare at Prince Albert and growled a low growl.

'Molly Malone,' repeated Hetty, 'you think you're the best sneak thief in Dublin, but I bet you're not as good as me at *anything*!' She pointed at the Test-Your-Strength machine, 'Let's have a go at this yoke, an' we'll see who's strongest!'

'The only strong thing about you is your smell, Hetty,' said Billy the Pan, who, to be honest, had a bit of a cheek – he wasn't the sweetest smelling person himself.

Hetty ignored him and furrowed her eyebrows and jutted out her chin in defiance, 'Well, what's the matter, Malone – are you too … chicken?'

Molly stepped forward and rolled up the silk sleeves of her fancy green dress, 'Let's do it, and we'll see who clucks first!'

The punters who had been waiting in line for the Test-Your-Strength machine backed away as the two fierce girls approached, and the machine's owner raised his hands. 'Now, look,' he said, 'I don't want any trouble!' Molly picked up the heavy wooden mallet with a grunt and held it high over her head. 'You won't … hear a … squeak of … trouble from me,' she said, and (with a small squeak) smashed the hammer down onto the dome. The arrow flew up to number SIX and the Spooks cheered and congratulated Molly, clapping her on the back as she panted with exertion.

Hetty picked up the mallet from where Molly had dropped it on the grass. In Hetty's hands the heavy wooden mallet seemed to be as light as a feather and several of the Spooks gulped; this wasn't looking good for Molly. Hetty tossed the mallet easily from one hand to the other, raised it above her head and with a mighty swing, thumped it down onto the wooden dome at the bottom of the machine. The red arrow swiftly flew up the pillar and reached number EIGHT easily. The Spooks didn't cheer this time, but Prince Albert barked and jigged up and down on his tiny, furry legs. Hetty, dusted some non-existent dust off the front of her grubby pinafore and nonchalantly inspected her filthy fingernails. 'See,' she said, 'I can't be beaten.'

'Ahhhh,' said Molly, still panting slightly after the effort, 'but being the best isn't all about brute strength. I challenge you to another competition; one that's all about nerve and character – one that's more about the strength of your mind rather than the strength of your back.' She pointed at the brightly painted targets that were set up in front of the next tent, 'This challenge will make you quiver!' Hetty looked at the Spooks in puzzlement, but they were all looking at each other in confusion too.

Only Bram was laughing, slapping his knees in mirth. 'Quiver!' he giggled, 'Like the pouch an archer carries his arrows in!' The Spooks still looked bewildered. 'Never mind,' said Bram, wiping tears from his eyes.

Molly and Hetty both took a bow and an arrow from a barrel placed a few metres away from the roped-off targets, while Bram gave the target range's owner a couple of pennies. The targets were painted with blue and red circles, with a black *bullseye* circle at the centre.

'Ladies first,' said Hetty to Molly with a sweep of her hand.

'Who are you callin' a lady?' said Molly, 'Dust before the broom – you go first, two arrows each – and we'll see who makes the clean sweep this time.'

Hetty stood in front of the target and placed the arrow on the bow. She drew back the bow's taut string and let the arrow fly. It hit the target in the blue circle, close enough to the bullseye. Bram squinted at the target. *Not a bad shot...* Hetty's second arrow hit the target a little closer to the centre than the first. She stood back and wiped her nose with her sleeve triumphantly. 'Beat that!' she snorted at Molly.

Molly took Hetty's place facing the target. She closed her eyes and breathed deeply for several seconds.

'Get on with it!' snarled Hetty impatiently. Molly smiled slightly, opened her eyes and drew back the bowstring. She let her first arrow fly and it whizzed off toward the target with a whooshing sound. A split-second later there was a THUNK followed by a BOINNGGGG as the arrow embedded itself in the precise centre of the bullseye. The Spooks jumped up and down, howling for joy. Hetty's mouth hung open; she had never witnessed such a perfect shot.

But Molly wasn't finished. Again, she closed her eyes and breathed deeply. Hetty said nothing this time, but gasped as Molly let her second arrow fly. It seemed to be heading straight for the centre of the bullseye again, but as it flew it seemed to swerve slightly. There was the sound of splitting wood as the metal tip of Molly's arrow hit the feathered end of Hetty's arrow and sheared it in two, right down the length of its long wooden shaft.

'A direct hit!' shouted Rose, and the Spooks danced for joy.

'Just like Robin Hood! Robin Hood did the same thing in the old story!' cried Bram. 'We should call

Molly *Robin Good,* 'cos she's so Good at Robbin'!' laughed Billy.

'The best sneak thief in Dublin!' chanted Shep, with Calico Tom in hysterics beside him, 'The best sneak thief in Dublin!'

Hetty slunk off in silence, with Prince Albert trailing behind her; both seemed to have their tails between their legs.

'Molly,' said Bram to his friend, his face a picture of awe, 'How did you do that?'

Molly winked, 'My pal Little Feather taught me how to shoot a bow an' arrow when I was in New York. I didn't spend all me time swannin' around in snooty restaurants, talkin' to snooty people, you know! I prefer to spend my time makin' friends with *real* people. Like Little Feather. We stayed with her family – she called them her 'tribe' – out in the forest, and she and her brothers taught me a few tricks about shootin' arrows and tamin' animals. I knew they'd come in handy one day!'

CHAPTER SIX:

THE RINGSEND RINGMASTER

IN WHICH THE SPOOKS HAVE A BIG TIME IN THE BIG TOP, AND
SANJIT FINDS THAT HIS LESS—THAN—AVUNCULAR UNCLE HAS
GONE ASTRAY

After all that excitement, Bram thought that the circus show itself might seem like a bit of an anti-climax, but he was proved to be much mistaken. Their seats were the best in the house — sorry, *tent* — right in the front row (*Knowing one of the stars of the show certainly has its privileges*, thought

Bram) and the show was SENSATIONAL! It started off with Mr Pablo Fanque himself, the famous British circus owner – and another gentleman of colour, noted a very happy Shep – introducing the Henderson Brothers who performed a dangerous and death-defying high-wire act. This was followed by a display of trained, dancing dogs that both pleased and excited Her Majesty; Rose had to hold tight on to her collar to stop her from jumping into the ring and joining in. There were clowns who rode around the ring in a red wagon with trick wheels that fell off one by one – it had a spring-loaded seat that sent the driver shooting into the air, sending the audience into hysterics. There were wobbly balancing acts, and there was a big brass band who played throughout, each wearing scarlet jacket, with golden buttons and braids.

Then came the act that the Spooks had been waiting for! Mr Pablo Fanque entered the ring to a crescendo of trumpet blasts. He raised his shiny top hat from his equally shiny bald head and ostentatiously twiddled his jet-black moustache. The circus lights bounced off the big golden buttons that paraded down the front of his red velvet frock coat like two straight lines of marching golden scarab beetles, and sparkled off the golden-fringed epaulettes on his shoulders.

'Ladies and Gentlemen!' he bellowed, his voice loud, rich and mellifluous, '*Mesdames et Messieurs*, or, as you say in Dublin City, Young Wans and Young Fellas! Let me introduce to you the greatest horseman in all the Americas, the most prodigious trickrider this side of the Mississippi and to the east of the Rio Grande, the astounding pony-vaulter extraordinaire – Mr Wild Bert Florence!'

Accompanied by another deafening fanfare of trumpets, Wild Bert rode into the ring, his white hat held high above his head. He was astride a huge white horse with a braided white mane and long, swishing white tail. The horse had a white leather saddle on its back, encrusted with blue jewels and rhinestones. 'Hi-yo, Buttercup!' yelled Bert, and the horse reared up on its two back legs in a salute to the spectators. The audience clapped and cheered, and Molly gave her signature whistle. Tipping his hat to The Sackville Street Spooks, Bert pulled a long silver gun from a holster he wore on his white leather belt and fired off a volley of loud, popping gunshots into the air above his head. There was a squawking noise and a crow tumbled from the top of the tent, landing at Buttercup's hooves with a crash and sending up a cloud of sawdust. The crowd gasped, but Wild Bert swung over on his saddle and nimbly grabbed the crow up by its feet. 'Don't worry,' he yelled, 'the bird isn't real – it's stuffed; and my bullet's ain't real neither, they're just blanks!' He tossed the stuffed crow to a waiting clown. 'Stick her in the oven, Bump-o, I'll have her for ma supper!' he said, then he gave a big theatrical wink, 'Just kiddin', folks!'

With a second cry of 'Hi-yo, Buttercup!' Bert launched into a series of amazing riding tricks that astounded the audience and had them up out of their seats clapping and stamping their feet. He rode Buttercup around the ring while standing on one leg on the horse's saddle. He juggled swords blindfolded on the horse while sitting backwards on her back. He used his gun to shoot a silver dollar off the brim of a pink hat worn by a very nervous looking Bump-o, all while Buttercup jumped over fences. He even did a trick where he got Buttercup to spell out her own name with her hoof in the dust of the Big Top floor.

'Here, Billy,' said Shep, 'That horsey can spell much better than you can!'

Billy the Pan smiled back at his pal, 'Shurrup, you.'

Then Bert announced his greatest trick: *The Absolutely Amazing & Unutterably Incredible Circus Royal Safari Leap.* Wild Bert rode around the ring in circles; on every completed circuit another large animal was let into the ring and joined in the chase. First of all an antlered stag joined Buttercup, then on the next circuit an African antelope arrived in. Next to join in was a black and white-striped zebra, and lastly in the middle, a tiny Shetland pony; each was wearing a rhinestone-encrusted leather saddle that glittered and shone in the circus lights. The five animals ran in concentric circles around the ring beside each other with Buttercup on the outside, sending up clouds of dust and seeming to go faster and faster with every revolution. Round and round they went until, with a loud cry of 'Hi-yo, Buttercup!' Bert launched himself off Buttercup's back and onto the back of the stag. Buttercup then left the ring and Bert jumped from the stag's back onto the saddle of the antelope. The stag left and Bert jumped from the antelope onto the zebra, who brayed loudly like a donkey. Finally, Bert sprung from the zebra's back and leapt right over the Shetland pony, landing in the centre of the ring. He took off his white cowboy hat and flung it in the direction of the tiny pony who slowed down as it trotted around the ring and came to a stop in the centre, wearing Bert's hat on its head. Wild Bert grabbed his hat from the Shetland pony's head, held his arms wide and fired his gun into the air. 'Can I get a YEEEEEE-HAAAAAWWWWWW?' he cried.

'YEEEEEE-HAAAAAWWWWWW!' shouted the crowd, on their feet, clapping and cheering as hard and loud as they could; but none of them were clapping harder or louder than the Spooks!

'Don't forget, folks,' shouted Wild Bill as he leaped onto the back of Buttercup and rode around the ring, taking in the crowd's applause, 'Mr Pablo Fanque's Travellin' Circus Royal will be appearin' again tomorrow – that's Monday night – at Donnybrook Field! See y'all there! Now, if you'll excuse me, I gotta go reward my amazin' animals with lots of tasty carrots! YEEEEEE-HAAAAAWWWWWW!'

* * *

When the circus ended, Billy had to return the buggy to where he *borrowed* it from. 'I better get poor Betty here back before they notice she's missing,' he said leading the horse and carriage off towards the City.

Molly, Bram, Shep and Sanjit walked across down Artichoke Road and over the bridge onto Grand Canal Street. They couldn't find Rose when they were leaving the circus tent, they had lost her somewhere in the crowd. 'Maybe she's waitin' around for Bert,' said Shep, looking left and right. 'Well, she's big enough to find her own way home,' said Molly, 'We have to get Sanjit back to the Museum.'

It was a short walk to Merrion Square in the early evening sunshine, but as they rounded the corner of the park, they could see a group of policemen milling around the Natural History Museum's door which, even though it was Sunday, was wide open. As they got to the entrance the doorman recognised

Sanjit and nodded to the policemen to let them in.

Inside the Museum was a picture of chaos. Policemen and staff were rushing around, some even bumping into each other as they bustled about ineffectively. An elderly gentleman was squinting short-sightedly through thick spectacles at wooden cases that had been overturned and poking shards of broken glass that lay about the floor with his walking stick.

'Doctor Travers,' said Sanjit to the worried-looking old man, 'what happened here?' Doctor Travers shook his head and led the children over to the display that held the bear and the rest of Captain Lamprey's menagerie of animals. Each of the animals – the moose, the mountain lion, the wolf, the big bear, even the crocodile – had been ripped open, their fur (or scales, in the case of the poor croc) hanging down in ragged flaps. Stuffing was falling out of each, and a small mountain range of the yellowing material had formed at their feet.

'The menagerie!' cried Sanjit, 'They were Uncle's favourites! What will Uncle Seth say!' Doctor Travers put his hand on the boy's shoulder. 'I hate to have to tell you this, my boy,' he said softly, 'but it seems your uncle can't be found. I was sitting down to luncheon this afternoon when I got a message that there were strange noises being heard coming from the Museum. I came to investigate, and when I opened the door I heard a voice – your uncle's voice, I believe – shouting for help, that he was being kidnapped! When I walked in, I found this mess and no sign of Professor Kumar. The side door was swinging open – that must have been how the gang of miscreants got in and out. Whoever did this to the poor stuffed animals must have taken your uncle! In all my years of being Master of the Museum, both here and in Leinster House, I've never beheld such a kerfuffle.' The elderly Doctor Travers sighed, 'I *do* hope your uncle is found, he sent such lovely letters before he arrived; of course, for such a tall man he is quite short in person, as you well know. *Short* as in *abrupt*, I mean. A-ha!' With that Doctor Travers limped back towards the puzzled policemen.

Sanjit staggered and sat down heavily on the floor. 'My goodness,' he said quietly, 'Uncle Seth can be strict with me sometimes – he shouts at me and scolds me when I do even the smallest wrong; he is so different to how my mother described him – but I never wished for my uncle to be kidnapped!'

As Molly knelt to comfort Sanjit, Bram inspected the damage to the stuffed animals. *Why would anyone rip these animals apart?* he wondered. *Was it just wilful destruction, just for the sake of it? Or were they perhaps looking for something that might be hidden inside?* He looked inside each animal in turn, noticing that under each animal's fur and stuffing there was a kind of metal skeleton that held the animal up, and that it was wired together in pieces to made them pose, just like they would in nature. He could see nothing at all that might be hidden in any of the animals. *Gosh*, he thought, *there isn't much room inside any of them to hide anything bigger than a piece of paper.*

The last animal he looked at was the big brown grizzly bear, standing with the little cub at its feet. The cub looked untouched, so Bram dragged a nearby wooden chair over so he could stand on it to look into the mama bear's poor sliced open body. *Empty, like the others.* But as he was getting down from the chair something caught his eye, a glint of light colour beneath the brown fur of the shoulder.

He stood back up on the chair and slid his hand down the neck of the bear, past the shoulder and into the arm. The metal skeleton made it tricky, but he managed to get his fingertips in as far as the light-coloured object hidden deep in the bear's arm and he began to slowly pull it out.

It was a very old piece of stiff, folded paper. Yellow with age and crumbling around the edges, it was covered in spidery writing with hand-drawn symbols and letters in faded black and red ink. Bram climbed down from the chair and carefully unfolded the fragile paper sheet. At the top was a symbol that made Bram gasp: a crudely drawn bear skull with two bones inked beneath it.

'The skull and cross bones!' whispered Shep excitedly, 'That's the Jolly Roger sign, except with a bear skull instead of a human one! Oh, Bram! Is this a – a pirate's treasure map?' At the mention of treasure, Molly and Sanjit jumped to their feet and crowded around the mysterious paper held in Bram's trembling hands.

'I don't know, Shep,' said Bram slowly, 'but I think we've found what the kidnappers were looking for!'

Just then there was a yell as Billy the Pan ran into the Museum, deftly sidestepping and weaving around the Peelers who tried to stop him. 'Molly!' he shouted, 'Bad news! Rose has been arrested for fighting with Hetty Hardwicke on Ringsend Green, and they've both been carted off to the Workhouse!'

Molly shook her head to clear it – so much was happening, and it all seemed to be happening at once! 'Alright,' she said, 'Billy, you and Shep will have to rescue Rose from the Workhouse.' She looked at Bram, 'Bram and me are going to help Sanjit find his uncle.'

'And,' added Bram, 'we are going to find out who in the world did this to Captain Lamprey's poor animals – and, more importantly, *why*.'

CHAPTER SEVEN

WILL THE REAL SHADY UNCLE PLEASE STAND UP? PLEASE STAND UP? PLEASE STAND UP?

IN WHICH THE REAL, ACTUAL, FACTUAL, GENUINE,
HONEST—TO—GERTRUDE UNCLE SETH MEETS HIS MATCH —
IN MORE WAYS THAN ONE

Uncle Seth sat in near-complete darkness on the cold, diamond-shaped red and black tiles, and looked down to his lap where he imagined his hands might be. He raised both to his mouth – he had to, they were tied together – and once again tried to bite his way through the ropes that bound his wrists. After four weeks of trying, he hadn't made much headway. Sighing with frustration he flopped back on the blanket that served as his bed and closed his eyes, thinking about how he had ended up here.

He had been so happy when he set out by ship from Bombay months before. As the ship set sail, crossing the Indian Ocean and rounding the Cape of Good Hope at the bottom of Africa (he had no idea that he was following the route taken by the infamous Captain Lamprey; it would have greatly amused him if he had), he reflected on how proud his family had been that he had firstly finished his education at the far-away University of Calcutta, working afterwards at the same University for several years, and then had been appointed to a prestigious job at the Natural History Museum in (much further-away) Dublin. He was the first member of the Kumar clan to visit Ireland; to work in its brand new, state-of-the-art Natural History Museum was such a great honour! Despite the turmoil in Bombay – a lot of ordinary Indian people were rebelling against British Rule, and it wasn't too safe to go out on the streets after dark – his family had thrown a small party for him the night before he left. At the party all the discussion was about the rebels and the fighting, and towards the end of the night his beloved sister Mina had asked him if he would be willing to take her son Sanjit with him to Ireland. 'It will be safer there, Seth,' she said, looking pleadingly at her brother, 'Let him stay with you even for a few weeks, just until the fighting is over.' Seth readily agreed; he hadn't seen his nephew since he was a tiny baby, he had been away in Calcutta for so long, but he was sure he could take care of a ten-year-old boy in Dublin – what loving uncle could refuse such a request? It was agreed that Seth would go ahead, and a servant would deliver Sanjit to him in Ireland after a week or so.

Once Seth reached London, he spent the afternoon filling his travelling trunk with books and jigsaws that he thought his nephew might like, and then that evening left his hostelry in search of food, and maybe a little celebratory orange juice to drink – it had been a very long voyage.

In a dingy tavern called *The Lamb and Flag* in Covent Garden, he chatted about Dublin to some Irish people at the bar, and then towards the end of the night fell in with a group of men from India. He traded stories about Bombay and Calcutta with them, and when they heard he was headed for Dublin, talk turned naturally to the old story of Captain Lamprey and the famous lost Rajapur Ruby. 'It's definitely in Dublin!' cried one man.

'That ruby is worth millions of rupees!' cried another, 'Millions!'

Seth laughed and shook his head. 'I'm afraid I don't know anybody in Dublin at all,' he said, 'but I will certainly ask about the whereabouts of the Rajapur Ruby as soon as I get there!'

Then another man, a tall, dark-haired fellow with a long black beard who had been listening silently to the conversation, seemed to become animated at the mention of the Ruby of Rajapur. He pushed his way to the centre of the crowd and spat out the tiny, smoky cigar stub he had clenched between his teeth.

With a glare around the crowd, he drained the dregs
of drink from his pint tankard and in a deep, tuneful
voice started to sing a sea shanty:

'There was a brave pirate ship set out to sea
Howl wind, bellow and growl
And the name of that ship was *The Menagerie*
With a bark and a squawk, a bellow and growl,'

'The sails were all set and with stars as our guide
Howl wind, bellow and growl
To the Indian Ocean we sailed at high tide
With a bark and a squawk, a bellow and growl,'

'Each cannon was manned by a hoof or a claw
Howl wind, bellow and growl
In the dead of the night, you could hear her
  crew call
With a bark and a squawk, a bellow and growl,'

'The first mate was a moose and the helmsman a bear
Howl wind, bellow and growl
In the crow's nest a crocodile peeped through the air
With a bark and a squawk, a bellow and growl,'

'We stole from the Sultan, a ruby renowned
Howl wind, bellow and growl
And hid it away where it will not be found
With a bark and a squawk, a bellow and growl,'

'My animals guard it, the ruby so fair
Howl wind, bellow and growl
If you should seek it, you'd better beware
Of the barks and the squawks, the bellows and growls.'

Some of the other men knew the song, although they hadn't heard it since they were children and couldn't remember all the words. They tried to join in on the 'Howl wind, bellow and growl' parts, but the singing was half-hearted and died out completely as the tall fellow's voice grew louder in the final verses.

'Captain Lamprey's Pirate Shanty,' said the tall man when he had finished the song. A couple of the men nodded and smiled at the strange, black-bearded character with the deep singing voice (and excellent memory for childhood shanties), and the man sat

down heavily again on his wooden stool and, clutching his empty pint tankard to his long black beard,
glared balefully in the direction of the professor.'

A little while later, Uncle Seth said his goodbyes
to his temporary acquaintances and took his leave of
the tavern. As he walked through the foggy London
streets back to his hostel, he didn't notice the tall
man following him.

The next morning Seth took the train to Liverpool, and from there boarded a steam ferry for the
short trip to Dublin. Once in Dublin, he made his
way to the Natural History Museum in Merrion
Square where, after a short meeting with the short-
sighted Master of the Museum, Doctor Travers, who
gave him a quick tour, he was shown his new basement living quarters.

'You'll be the only one living on-site, old boy,'
said the elderly Doctor, squinting at Seth through
very thick spectacles, 'I hope you won't be *too* lonely.
A-ha!'

Seth replied that he wouldn't, his nephew would
be joining him shortly, and bid the myopic Travers
a good night. He then packed away the contents of

his travelling trunk, and went out to get something to eat.

He marvelled at the green-tinged beauty of Dublin City as he made his way back in the moonlight after dinner to the now empty Museum; Dublin seemed so different from Bombay, and yet so similar in many ways. He was reaching up to put his key into the keyhole of the side entrance when he heard a grunt behind him and felt a sharp bang across the back of his head.

The next thing he knew ... he was here – tied up in almost pitch darkness. He had tried shouting for help, but had received no answer. Wherever he was being kept, the walls must be very thick, almost soundproofed. Twice a day, a man, his face shrouded in shadow, opened the door, left a plate of food on the floor and changed the chamber pot. Seth had tried shouting for help then, as well as asking the man where he was and why he had been imprisoned here, but no answer came to either question – other than the man putting his finger to his lips and quietly closing and locking the door again, leaving a whiff of pungent cigar smoke lingering in his wake. Although he could only see the man in silhouette, Seth thought there was something very familiar about this stranger, with his tall frame and his long beard. He couldn't help thinking he had met this man before ...

* * *

The man scowled into his pint tankard as he listened to this so-called 'professor' bragging about how he was going to work in some Museum or other in Dublin. 'The Natural History Museum,' the professor had said, 'the place where they display the stuffed animals.' The tall man had no time for animals, stuffed or otherwise. He only had time for money, but unfortunately for the man, he didn't have very much of that. He checked his pockets for another coin with which to buy another drink, but every pocket was empty. He sat back on his wooden stool and half-listened as the talkative professor droned on. And on. And on ...

His ears pricked up though when he heard a familiar name: Captain Lamprey. And his eyes opened wide as he heard three very familiar words: The Rajapur Ruby. *The ruby that was stolen from the Sultan of Rajapur by the dread pirate Lamprey? Why, every Bombay child knows that story! And this man is saying that he will be working in the very Museum where Captain Lamprey's infamous stuffed animal crew are on display?* The man's mind, now fully awake, sprang into action like wound-up clockwork. *What was that old song? I learnt it at my grandmother's knee, every other kid in Bombay probably learned it at their grandmother's knee too. It was called … Captain Lamprey's Pirate Shanty!*

As much to remind himself of the words as anything else, the man found himself standing up and starting to sing. As the verses went on and he remembered the words, his voice got louder and louder. Everyone in the tavern was staring at him. Those who had joined in on the call-and-repeat verse ending of 'Howl wind, bellow and growl' had fallen silent, but he didn't care – he had to get to the end. The clue was at the end of the song, he was sure of it!

'My animals guard it, the ruby so fair
Howl wind, bellow and growl

If you should seek it, you'd better beware
Of the barks and the squawks, the bellows and growls.'

'My animals guard it!' It was right there in the song!
The ruby is guarded by the animals! The animals
who are residing in the very Museum where this
idiot professor is going to be working! The man sat
back down on the wooden stool and stared at the
professor as he resumed the friendly conversation
he had been having with his Indian countrymen.
The professor was tall with a long, black beard. The
tall man on the stool looked down at his own long,
black beard. He furrowed his jet black, bristling eyebrows and raised his head to stare at the professor.
In Dublin, he thought to himself, *surely nobody knows
what this man looks like – he says himself he knows no
one there. Perhaps one tall man with a long, black beard
could be easily mistaken for another tall man with a long,
black beard by these idiots in Dublin?*

When the professor left the tavern, the man stood
up and followed him. When Sanjit's Uncle Seth left
his hostel the next morning and caught the train to
Liverpool, the tall man got into the next carriage

along. When the professor boarded the ferry for the short trip to Dublin, the man walked up the gang-plank three steps behind him. And when poor Uncle Seth came back from his dinner and put his key into the keyhole at the side door of the Museum, it was the bearded man's iron bar that smacked him hard across the back of the head.

The tall, bearded man dragged Seth's unconscious body into the Museum and down the steps to the basement. At the end of the corridor where Seth's rooms were, the man found another set of steps that led down into a sub-basement, and there he tied up the poor professor and locked him into a disused storeroom.

The man climbed the stairs to Seth's basement living quarters and tried on his clothes. They fitted! Gazing at his reflection in a mirror, the tall man thought he looked rather dashing in the professor's tweed suits and fashionable top hats – the clothes fitted so well that he and the professor could be twin brothers! He had fed and cleaned out the idiot professor twice a day while he bided his time, waiting for the right moment to properly investigate Lamprey's stuffed animal crew – it had been surprisingly easy to act like a real professor with the other staff, and he had been right in his assumption that to the Museum staff who had only met the professor briefly, one bearded academic would look much like any other bearded academic.

The only fly in the ointment had been the unexpected arrival after the first week of the child Sanjit, the professor's nephew, although the man had easily fooled him too. It was lucky that Sanjit hadn't seen his uncle since he was a baby and had no real memory of him. His mother had told the child to expect someone tall with a beard, and that was who greeted Sanjit on his arrival at the Museum – a tall man with a beard. Who was Sanjit to say that this man wasn't his uncle? Even if Sanjit had suspicions, (which he didn't) who would have believed him? He was a child after all, and children, in the tall man's opinion, were all idiots.

So the tall, bearded man had duped Sanjit, and had stolen Uncle Seth's freedom as well as his identity. All that was left was to get his hands on Lamprey's stuffed animals, and now that Sanjit was making friends – something that the tall man (posing as his Uncle Seth) had expressly forbidden him to do – the man knew that his time was short. He had to act *now*.

The very next morning the man's chance had come – Sanjit had escaped for the day; the man had heard him sneaking out of the Museum and had watched from a window as his 'nephew' had gotten into a carriage and was driven away. The Museum was empty, and the tall man was alone. He threw the stub of his half-smoked cigar onto the red and black tiled floor and stubbed it out viciously with the heel of his shoe. The man went down to the sub-basement room and slid a plate of food across the floor towards the real Uncle Seth, who shouted for help again (as if any was coming), then the tall man locked the door and climbed the stairs.

He walked across the silent, deserted Museum towards the glass display case in which Captain Lamprey's animal crew stood, and looked in turn at the wolf, the two bears, the mountain lion, the moose, and the ridiculous-looking one-armed croc-odile. The man picked up heavy wooden chair and swung it hard at the glass. The thunderous sound of smashing glass echoed around the tall walls of the Museum, bouncing off the mezzanines and reverberating around the balconies, but nobody was there to hear it. Except for the tall man.

With his small feet swimming in the real Uncle Seth's long, brown, brogue-style shoes, the man crunched over thousands of shards of broken glass and stepped up into the wooden case where Lamprey's animals were lined up in a row, the way they used to stand guard on the deck of *The Menagerie*. The poor animals seemed to stare at the tall, bearded man accusingly, as from the inside of his coat, he pulled out a long, razor-sharp knife and went to work …

Chapter Eight

Captain Lamprey's
Confusing Clues

In which Molly and Bram peruse a pirate map, and pursue a pirate's treasure

ram, Molly and Sanjit sat around the large dinner table in Bram's family dining room at 19 Buckingham Street, with a map of Dublin spread out before them. Molly was holding old piece of paper they had found in Captain Lamprey's bear and was squinting at it in the gaslight, trying to decipher the old writing.

They had arrived at the house a couple of hours earlier and Bram's mother, on seeing that Bram had his friends with him, immediately welcomed them in and ordered Lily the maid to lay extra places for dinner at the dining table. Bram's father was a little concerned to see a scruffy-looking dog trot into his lovely, clean, neat and tidy house, but Lily took a shine to Her Majesty, brushing her fur and making her look pretty by tying a bow in the fur at the top of her doggy head.

Once the children had washed their hands and tidied their hair to Mama Stoker's satisfaction, they sat down to a scrumptious dinner of roast pork with potatoes, creamed cauliflower and buttered green beans, served up to them by the hardworking maid. A smiling Sanjit politely declined the pork, he had never eaten it before, but he assured Bram's mother that he would be delighted to eat the vegetables.'

There was so much food on the table that it seemed to bow in the middle with the weight. 'Janey Mack, Quality,' Molly whispered to Bram as Mama

Stoker shovelled a third helping of cauliflower onto her plate, 'Do you eat like this every day?'

Bram shook his head. 'Only on Sundays ...' he whispered with a smile.

'Absolutely tickety-boo delicious!' declared Molly in her best simulated-snooty accent.

It was agreed that the children would stay that night in the Stoker house – Molly's uncle – the fictional one with the large estate with all the horses at the Curragh of Kildare – had unfortunately broken the fictional wheel on his fictional carriage, so couldn't collect her and her friend Sanjit this evening.

'No matter, I simply *adore* entertaining guests,' trilled Mama Stoker, 'especially unexpected ones! There are plenty of guest rooms ... and more than enough food to go around!'

No kidding, thought Molly, *their pantry must be the size of The Sackville Street Spooks' old shack!*

At the end of the meal, Lily the maid appeared to clear away the plates and Molly, of course, insisted on helping her. 'We are all used to mucking in on the horse farm,' she explained to an astonished Mama Stoker, 'Mucking *out* too!' Telling the children not to stay up *too* late, Bram's mama and papa then retired across the wide, comfortably carpeted hallway to the sitting room, and Bram turned up the gas lamps and began to search through the bookcases that lined one wall of the dining room. He found what he was looking for, took it down and spread it open on the dining table. 'Messrs Hardiman & Braithwaite's Patented Map of Dublin City,' said Bram, smoothing out the creases in the large map, 'It's the 1858 edition, but most of the streets should be the same as those in Captain Lamprey's time – it can't have changed all that much.'

'Good thinking,' said Molly, and unfolded the yellowing piece of paper she had kept hidden in the folds of her green dress. She looked at her new friend Sanjit. He was sitting at the end of the table with his hands in his lap and a sad look on his face. Molly had noticed that while she and Bram had tucked in hungrily to their dinner, Sanjit had barely touched any of his food. 'Don't worry, Sanjit,' she said, 'we will find your uncle for you. If this piece of paper is what the kidnappers were looking for, then we should follow the clues Captain Lamprey left for us

– if we do that, the kidnapper might give themselves away. Then we have a chance of finding your uncle, and maybe even find the treasure too!'

Sanjit brightened a little at that, glad to have a task to take his mind off his uncle's disappearance. He found Uncle Seth to be a scary, disagreeable character, but he *was* his mother's brother after all, and Sanjit didn't want anything bad to happen to him. Well, nothing *too* bad anyway.

They put the ancient piece of paper down on top of the map of Dublin. The paper had writing on both sides of the sheet, seeming random letters of the alphabet written in black and red ink in spidery, old-fashioned handwriting. A series of lines of connecting blocks that might have been streets or buildings covered the bottom half on one side, but they didn't seem to correspond to any street layout that Bram was familiar with. A handwritten letter *N* was at the right-hand side of the blocks. Bram looked at the Dublin map and then back to the pirate map again and again, but couldn't manage to make out any similarities between them at all.

At the top of the sheet was the bear skull and cross

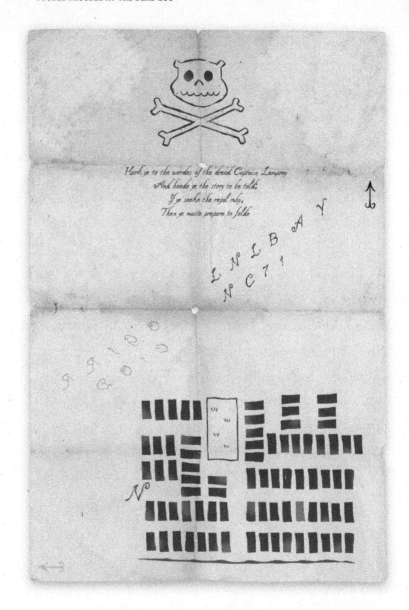

Hark ye to the wordes of the dread Captain Lamprey
And heede ye the story to be tolde;
If ye seeke the regal ruby,
Then ye muste prepare to folde

L N L B A Y
N C 7 1

bones – the Jolly Roger pirate symbol that the children had seen earlier – and beneath that a couple of sentences, written in tiny letters. Bram squinted at the paper to read the words. 'It's too dark in here,' he said, 'Treasure hunting should be done by daylight!' He picked up the paper and brought it closer to one of the hissing, wall-mounted gas lamps that jutted out of each wall.

'Hark ye to the wordes of the dread Captain Lamprey,' he read, then shook his head, 'I can't read the rest, it's too small.'

Molly appeared beside him holding a magnifying glass, 'Maybe this might help?' She took the page from her friend and squinted through the glass at the miniscule message. 'Hark ye to the wordes of the dread Captain Lamprey,' she read, 'and heede ye the story to be told; if ye seeke the regal ruby, then ye muste prepare to folde.'

'Prepare to fol-de?' said Bram, scratching his head, 'What does that mean? His spelling is atrocious, by the way.' He put the paper down on the table again and stared at it. There was a line of letters and numbers in black ink climbing across the page at an angle on one side: L, N, L, B, A, Y, N, C, 7, 1. He turned the page over. On the other side was another angled line of letters and numbers written in red ink: O, G, I, R, R, C, 1, 0, D. There was an old-fashioned arrow at opposite sides of the page, one red and one in black ink. Bram held the paper up again to the light. It was heavy enough, but even so he could just make out the shadows of the letters written on the other side.

'Fold!' cried Sanjit suddenly, jumping up from his place at the end of the table, 'Not "fol-de"! His spelling isn't atrocious, it's just old-fashioned!' He grabbed the paper from Bram, 'What if that means we have to "folde"'the paper?'

'Yes!' said Molly, 'And if you hold it up to the gas light, you can see through to what's written on the other side – maybe some of these letters might join up and start to make sense.'

Bram folded the paper in half and held it up to the light again. The jumbled letters on either side didn't line up at all.

'What about folding it diagonally to make the two arrows meet?' suggested Sanjit, pointing at the red and black arrows on either side. Bram folded the paper crossways so that the tip of the red arrow on one side met the tip of the black arrow on the other and held it up to the gas lamp. Molly gasped.

'L. O. N. G. L. I. B. R. A. R. Y. N. C. C. 1. 7. 0. 1. D.' she read, 'What's a long library?'

'The Long Room!' cried Bram.

'The Library in Trinity College! You are right!' beamed Sanjit, 'That must be where the Ruby is!'

'Or at least another clue as to where it might be …' said Bram, 'But what do the other letters and numbers mean? NCC and 1701D – they don't make any sense.'

Molly frowned, 'Maybe they'll make more sense once we get to the Library.'

Bram glanced at the clock on the mantelpiece, it was already a quarter past eight. 'Well, we aren't going to the library right now,' he said, folding up Captain Lamprey's map again and putting it carefully into the inside pocket of his jacket, 'it's too late to do anything else at all tonight; I suggest we go to bed and have a good night's rest.'

'Another good idea, Quality,' said Molly. 'And tomorrow we will go to this Trinity College Long

Room Library, follow Captain Lamprey's clues, find the Rajapur Ruby and rescue Sanjit's uncle!' She winked at Bram and Sanjit, 'Easy peasy!'

* * *

The tall, bearded man stroked his black moustache thoughtfully as he stood in the shadow of a tree and stared up at the dining room window of 19 Buckingham Street. Seeing the three children inside standing up from the table, he stepped back, covering the red glow from the lit tip of his cigar with his hand, and making sure he was far enough away from the oval of yellow light from the street gas lamps that he couldn't be seen. The light went out in the dining room and the house became dark and silent.

They've gone to bed, he thought, his eyes on the front of number 19, *there won't be any move from them until the morning.* He sat on the step of the building opposite the Stoker house and settled in for the night.

It was a stroke of genius on his part, he thought, to call out that he was being kidnapped when he realised that he was about to be discovered. He had been searching Captain Lamprey's animals in search of the legendary Ruby of Rajapur, or failing that, some sort of clue to its whereabouts – ripping the stuffed animals open with his razor-sharp blade, pulling the fur back, tearing out the stuffing and peering inside each – but he had seen nothing out of the ordinary in any of them, certainly no sign of the Rajapur Ruby or anything like it. Each animal had a metal skeleton and was filled with dry, light-yellow stuffing. The man thought it might have been horsehair, but what did he know about animals? He was only *pretending* to be a professor of animal biology.

Then, as he sliced open the big grizzly bear from the neck to the belly, pulling back its fur and looking inside, he spotted a light-coloured object stuffed down inside the bear's arm, just beyond the shoulder joint. He put his knife between his gleaming teeth and tried to insert his fingers into the narrow space inside the arm to retrieve whatever it was – could it have been a piece of old paper? – but his hands were just too big. He had taken the knife from between his teeth again to tear at the fur of the arm when he heard a noise behind him; the sound of a key turning in a lock! His head shot around, and he saw the tall door of the Museum being pushed open, and slivers of early evening light seeping into the darkened Museum from around the edges. He took one last longing look at the piece of mysterious paper secreted inside the bear's arm – *so near and yet so far!* – and then took a deep breath. He didn't know what he was going to shout before he opened his mouth wide; to his surprise, what came out was, 'Help! Someone help me! I'm being kidnapped!'

Knife in hand, he jumped out of the display case and bolted like a racehorse for the side door. He threw the door open and threw himself through it. The tall man sprinted for the safety of the trees in the Merrion Square Park, practically running up and over the fence, until his body was completely concealed by the bushes beyond.

From his hidden vantage point, he waited and watched as the police arrived, and then observed the four idiot children as they returned from wherever it was that children went. He saw that his own nephew – well, not his nephew, but the brat he was *pretending* to be the uncle of – was with the other children. He was hoping that neither the doorman nor the police would notice the strange piece of paper hidden inside the arm of the big grizzly bear. *But then again,* he thought, *why would they? Police are idiots after all; they have no more common sense than idiot children.* He was most surprised then, to find three *idiot* children, his fake nephew included, leaving the Museum a few minutes later in a state of excitement. As they walked, the two boys crowded around the red-haired girl in the green dress, who seemed to be holding a very old, yellowing piece of paper!

The tall man's eyes narrowed. That piece of paper was *his*; he had found it fair and square! And any clues that might be written on it belonged to him and him alone! *He* would be the one to find this treasure!

He watched as the children and their dog rounded the corner and then decided to do what he did best – follow them. He tracked the children to the Stoker house on Buckingham Street, where they had eaten dinner, inspected the map (or whatever it was) after the plates had been cleared, and now had gone to bed.

The man pulled his knees up to his chin and tried

to make himself more comfortable on the step, all the while keeping his beady, greedy eyes on the house opposite. He thought momentarily about the *real* Uncle Seth, tied up in the sound-proof sub-basement back at the Museum. The *real* Seth would be wondering where the man who gave him his food twice a day had gone. With the police looking anywhere else but the basement of the Museum for the *fake* kidnapped Uncle, it may be quite a while before the *real* Uncle Seth was discovered – poor Uncle Seth might have missed a great many meals by then. This thought made the tall man happy, and he stifled a giggle as he shifted on the step. *Better get comfortable,* he thought to himself, *it's going to be a long night, and I won't be getting much sleep.*

The Diary of Master Abraham Stoker
Sunday 20th of March, 1859
19 Buckingham Street, Dublin

Dearest Diary,
Of all the things I imagined myself to be doing tomorrow, on the first real day of my mid-term

break from school, I never thought I would be following the clues on a hundred-year-old pirate map in search of a priceless, legendary lost ruby, not to mention attempting to draw out the kidnappers of a visiting professor from India!

With all this excitement, I can barely contemplate the idea of sleeping – my mind races so! But sleep I must, if I am to be entirely ready and fully prepared for any and all further adventures that tomorrow may hold.

And whatever about the Rajapur Ruby, I just hope we can find Sanjit's uncle.

My, though, the adventures I am having! I am sure to be a writer when I am older!

Until tomorrow then, dearest Diary, I remain your faithful friend,

Bram

CHAPTER NINE:

ALL IN A DAY'S WORKHOUSE

IN WHICH BILLY THE PAN AND SHEP GO UNDERCOVER TO LIBERATE
A LOAD OF LOCKED–UP LABOURERS

'Ah, Janey,' said Shep, looking at himself in the window of a fishmonger's shop on Thomas Street; it had been raining all day and the water running down the window glass distorted his reflection, 'Do I have to wear this yoke? I look like a right eejit.'

Billy the Pan looked his smaller pal up and down, and smirked. Shep was completely correct, he did

150

look like a bit of an eejit. But then again, so did Billy. Both boys were wearing long rough white cotton work dresses over blue and white-striped blouses – the uniform of the dreaded South Dublin Work-house. On each boy's head was a frilly maid's white cap and on their feet were scuffed brown leather sandals fastened with copper buckles.

'Sorry they're not the cleanest of clothes,' Billy had said earlier that afternoon when he presented the bundle of clothes to Shep, 'but when I broke into the laundry earlier I couldn't find the hampers with the clean uniforms in them; I took these out of the to-be-washed pile – just stick them on over your normal clothes.'

Now, regarding his friend as Shep adjusted the frilly cap to completely hide his very short, curly black hair, Billy had to smile again. 'If it makes any difference, Shep, I think you actually look quite good in a dress,' he said.

'Hmmmm,' replied Shep, still slightly unsure of his new look, 'Right, what's the plan?'

'Molly's the one for making plans,' said Billy, slightly apologetically, 'but this is what I have so far

– One: we dress up in Workhouse uniforms. Two: we go up to the Workhouse, sneak in and find Rose.'

'And THREE?' asked Shep, not entirely unreasonably.

'I hadn't got as far as THREE yet,' said Billy, 'Like I said, Molly is the plannin' person. We will just have to make it up as we go along.'

Shep sighed and looked at himself in the wet shop windows as they walked past; despite the pouring rain he reflected that his reflection actually didn't look too bad at all. 'You know what?' he said, 'I *do* look pretty. Much prettier that you anyway, Billy – you have a moustache!' Billy shifted the cloth sack he was carrying from one hand to the other and bending, scooped a little wet mud off the ground with his fingers. Winking at his pal, he smeared the muck onto his top lip to better hide the light outcrop of whiskers that was starting to grow there.

They continued up Thomas Street and onto James Street where the South Dublin Workhouse stood. The building was tall and imposing, built with huge bricks of bleak grey granite that looked damp and cold in the rainy Monday downpour. It was built specially to house the destitute of Dublin; the poor and penniless who had no homes, no prospects and no hope. There were so many luckless people living in poverty that when they built the Workhouse, they built it big. In fact, the South Dublin Workhouse was the biggest Workhouse in Ireland.

It wasn't exactly a prison; but if you were unfortunate enough to end up there, you couldn't exactly just leave. The inmates, as the name of the South Dublin Workhouse suggests, were required to *work*. The men and boys did hard labour, much like they would in a real prison – breaking and grinding stones, and grinding bones for soup (there was always a lot of grinding involved); the women and girls did what was considered more 'ladylike' work – sewing and mending clothes, spinning wool or repairing shoes.

Billy had known many people who had ended up in the Workhouse; some poverty-stricken, famished families actually went there by choice, deciding it was better to be worked to near-death in the Workhouse than to starve to death in the streets. The police routinely sent street children and orphans to the Workhouse, sometimes for the smallest of offences, and most of The Sackville Street Spooks had spent stretches there at one time or another.

Molly's poor parents had both perished in the Workhouse on Constitution Hill on the other side of the Liffey, leaving her all alone and without a family. That was why, thought Billy, she had made a family of her own from scratch: the Sackville Street Spooks. That gang of kids – himself, Shep, Calico Tom, Rose, even Master Bram Stoker – were like brothers and sisters; they all looked out for one another. When one Spook was in trouble, the other Spooks rode in to the rescue.

And that was what he and Shep were doing right now: riding in to the rescue. Billy the Pan didn't mind that he was wearing a dress, ridiculous buckled shoes and an even more ridiculous frilly maid's hat, and neither did Shep. One of his family needed him, and he would do whatever it took to help.

Hold on, Rose, thought Billy, *The Spooks are on their way!* He lifted the frilly cap and scratched his head underneath with grimy fingernails. *Although this maid's cap is very itchy – I do miss wearing my good old saucepan on me head.*

The two boys walked by the main door of the Workhouse and made their way around the walls to the orchard that they knew lay behind the main building. Both had climbed the orchard wall before to strip the trees of apples and pears, Billy throwing the fruit over to Shep who waited on the other side, filling a wicker basket while he kept one watchful eye on the Workhouse door.

The wall to the orchard was easy enough to get over, even though the stones were slippery because of the rain, but the top of the wall was festooned with pieces of broken glass, sharp and cruel, to deter that very activity. Billy had worried that the glass might catch on the fabric of their long dresses and slow them down, but Shep had thought to bring along a thick doormat that Billy was able to throw up onto the wall, covering the worst of the glass shards. Billy went first, hefting his sack and pulling Shep up behind him, and soon they found themselves standing on the other side of the wall, their fancy-sandalled feet on soft, wet orchard grass, surrounded by trees. Buds and blossoms were sprouting on the branches, each glistening prettily with raindrops, but Shep was disappointed to realise that no fruit was on offer yet.

As they crept through the orchard towards the main building of the Workhouse, a bell sounded inside. 'Perfect timing,' whispered Billy, 'that should be the two o'clock dinner bell; all the girls should be troopin' out of the work hall now to go to the dinin' hall for their milk and spuds. Keep an eye out for Rose!'

At the Workhouse the inmates were worked very hard, rising at six o'clock in the morning and labouring until nine at night; but they were also fed three times a day. The meals were simple and small – a thin porridge gruel made of oatmeal and water for breakfast, a couple of sparse boiled potatoes and milk for dinner, and a piece of stale, dry bread for supper – but it was more food than most families could expect to get if they were so poor that they were reduced to living rough on the cold cobblestones of Dublin. To some people, slightly mouldy potatoes and the-day-before-yesterday's milk was practically a feast fit for Queen Victoria herself.

'There she is!' hissed Shep, pointing at the line of

unfortunate female inmates filing out into the rain through the shed-like doors of the work hall. Around fifty girls and women were in the line and Rose was halfway down the queue, walking beside a girl whose bushy hair was sticking out at all angles from beneath her frilly maid's cap.

'Great,' replied Billy the Pan, 'now we just have to—'

'What are you doing out of line?' roared a deep voice from behind them, making them both jump. They turned to find the biggest woman either of them had ever seen glowering down at them. The woman wore a brown suit of rough material, military in style, with brass buttons marching down the overstuffed chest and two circles of gold braiding stitched to the cuff of each sleeve. At the tightly buttoned up neck of the suit's jacket, a snow-white frilly collar supported a round, beetroot-red face topped with a slicked-down head of brown hair that looked almost like it had been painted on. Impervious to the rain, she held a folded-up umbrella under her elbow like a sergeant-major's swagger stick. 'Stand to attention when I speak to you!' she bellowed, her large face turning an even deeper shade of scarlet.

'Yes, Miss!' said Billy and Shep together, both standing straight and snapping to attention despite themselves.

'And address me as MATRON! My name is not Miss!' she boomed.

'Yes, Matron!' shouted Shep and Billy. Shep actually saluted! 'Sorry, Matron,' began Billy, 'we just–'

'I DON'T WANT TO HEAR YOUR EXCUSES!' thundered Matron, 'Get in line and get your potatoes, and then GET BACK TO WORK!!' She pointed a ramrod straight arm toward the line of women filing into the dining hall. Billy and Shep saluted again and trotted off to join the queue. Looking at them suspiciously, the Matron sniffed and turned on her heel in a very military manner, and marched off towards the main Workhouse building.

Inside the dining hall were four long tables with wooden benches on either side. The room itself was drab, with no pictures or decorations on the grey walls. The only light came in from slitted windows positioned high up on each wall, and a couple of candles on each table. The female inmates were standing in line at the top of the room, where each was receiving a small bowl of boiled potatoes and a chipped mug of milk. Once they had these, they sat at one of the long tables and started to eat enthusiastically. Some smacked their lips as if the plain potatoes and watered-down milk were the tastiest things they had had in their whole lives. And for some of them, thought Billy, that might have been true. Some of the women here were old enough to remember the Great Hunger of a few years before – when a series of severe potato blights spoiled the only food the poor could afford to eat, and caused widespread disease and death amongst the plain people of Ireland – so the steady supply of humble spuds they got daily in the Workhouse probably made them feel like they were eating like the Quality

Billy thought back to the feasts The Spooks had shared in their tumbledown shack at the side of the Royal Canal at Newcomen Bridge. They never had much to eat – they had to steal to be able to afford any food they got, swapping stolen silk handkerchiefs and hooky lace handbags in exchange for tiny roast chickens and minute slices of beef from the good people at nearby Mud Island. But as miniscule as their meals might have been, as least the food was tasty – this forgettable fare of potatoes and milk that the unfortunate Workhouse inmates were currently devouring with delectation was just, in Billy's opinion, too *bland* to be bothered with.

Despite that, Billy and Shep queued up with the others and got their mug and bowl. After a quick scan around the hall Shep tugged at the sleeve of Billy's work dress and pointed to a spot halfway down the third table. The she was, sitting beside the bushy-haired girl! They sidled down between the benches and with a couple of 'Excuse mes' and 'Beg yer pardons' plonked themselves down beside Rose and her pal.

Rose looked up from her almost-eaten bowl of potatoes and grinned. 'I wondered when you'd get here,' she said, popping the last potato in her mouth and finishing off her milk, 'I'm glad to see you both, even if you did take your own sweet time getting here.' Billy took a look at his bowl of spuds and pushed it away untouched, 'It just took a while to get my hands on the appropriate costume.'

'Well, I think the two of yiz look only gorgeous,'

said the bushy-haired girl.

'Hetty Hardwicke!' exclaimed Shep, 'What are you doing here? And what are you doin' sittin' beside Rose, as if you two are best friends in the whole world?'

'We *are* friends,' said Rose, 'I know we were picked up by the Peelers for fighting at the fair–'

Hetty put her hand on Rose's arm. 'Yeah, sorry about that,' she said. 'But we realised when we both ended up in here that we should work together,' continued Rose. 'Hetty's not too bad. In fact, she's just like us. She was tellin' me all about what happened years ago to her ma and da.'

'Why? What happened, Hetty?' asked Billy.

'That's the thing,' said Hetty, 'I don't know what happened to them.' She sighed and licked the last of the potato crumbs off her fingers, 'You see, I never knew 'em. I started life here in the Workhouse. Well, not this one, the North Dublin Workhouse.' Billy gulped; that was the one that Molly parents had died in.

'I was a foundling, an abandoned baby. I was left in a doorway on Henrietta Street, all alone and wrapped up in old newspapers and a raggy blanket,' said Hetty, 'When I was handed over to the police I was brought straight to the Workhouse. The Peeler who brought me in couldn't give my name at the desk – I didn't have a name – and he couldn't remember if I was found on Henrietta Street or Hardwicke Street, so the desk clerk wrote down my name in the admissions book as Henrietta Hardwicke. Hetty for short!'

'Please to meet you, Hetty!' said Shep, and stuck out his hand. Hetty shook it gratefully.

'I escaped from the Workhouse when I was old enough to walk,' Hetty continued, 'But they always manage to find me and bring me back.'

'Well, Hetty,' said Billy the Pan, 'are you ready for another escape?' Hetty grinned and nodded, 'That sounds good to me!'

'DINNER TIME IS OVER!' boomed a very familiar voice from behind the four children, 'GET BACK TO WORK!!' The Matron stood with her muscular arms folded and watched as the inmates, Rose, Hetty, Billy and Shep included, stood and filed out of the dining hall. Her thick eyebrows furrowed and she stared at the four children suspiciously.'

The work hall was three times the size of the dining hall, but was even more drab and gloomy, if that were possible. Rows of wooden tables filled the warehouse-like room, and the inmates sat at them in groups of six or eight. Many of the women were making repairs to fancy clothes – velvet jackets, lace petticoats and silk frocks – that the well-to-do people of Dublin had left in to be mended. More of the ladies appeared to be making brand-new uniforms for new Workhouse inmates who hadn't arrived yet (but given the abject poverty in many parts of inner-city Dublin, definitely would be coming). Around three sides of the enormous room were spinning wheels, where women and girls sat spinning yarn and wool. At the far end of the room were tall double doors that hung open. Steam gushed through this wide doorway and clanging noises could be heard from within.

Rose led Billy and Shep to a wooden table where she, the boys and Hetty sat down beside two other young girls, both of whom looked up and smiled shyly at the newcomers.

'We're meant to be fixin' these shoes,' said Rose,

pointing at a pile of worn and scuffed leather shoes and boots on the table. The two other girls returned to their work; one was using blacking to polish a pair of newly-mended shoes, the other was sewing splits in a delicate pair of ladies boots with waxed thread.

'Says your aul' one to my aul' one, "Will you go to the Waxies' Dargle?"' sang Shep softly.

'Shush your singin', Shep, will ya?' whispered Billy, 'We don't want to draw attention to ourselves. You just pretend to be working on these boots while I work on how to get us out of here!'

'Get us out of here?' repeated one of the other girls at the table, putting down the boot she was working on. 'Here, if you're all gettin' out, you're bringin' us with you!'

Billy the Pan scanned the room; he looked down at the uniform dress he was wearing and then looked over at the steam pouring out of the double doors at the end of the room. An idea slowly formed in his mind. 'Is that the laundry room over there, by any chance?' he asked the girl holding the shoe and the pot of blacking. She gave him a puzzled look and nodded her head. Billy took a look around to make sure nobody, especially the Matron, was watching them. 'Great,' he said, 'hand me that pot of shoeshine and I'll tell you what to do.'

A few seconds later the white uniform dress of every girl (and two boys) at Rose's table was covered with large daubs of shoe blacking, making the girls look more like spotty Dalmatian dogs than Work-house inmates.

'AAAAHHHHHH!' cried Rose, who knew how to cause a good diversion when the occasion demanded it, 'Hetty's after coverin' all our lovely dresses with this black shoe polish muck!!'

'HENRIETTA HARDWICKE!' roared the Matron, marching over to their table with a face like thunder, 'AND ROSE KELLY! What have I told the two of you about fighting!' She pointed her ramrod straight arm at the double doors and shouted orders at them like a Dragoon Guard drill sergeant. 'Get into the laundry this instant, put those dirty clothes into the wash and get changed!' she boomed, 'Bring these other girls with you! NOW!!'

'Yes, Matron!' shouted Rose and Hetty together, then, under the watchful eye of the Matron, they led the rest of the children to the end of the room and through the doors.

The laundry was warm inside. Through clouds of steam Billy could see big vats of hot, grey, sudsy water where women swished clothes around with big poles like oars from a canal barge. There was a long fireplace to one side where irons hung over the flames from metal rods to heat, and beside the fire there was a row of ironing boards, each with an inmate busy ironing the newly washed clothes. Clean, neatly folded uniforms were piled up on the floor beside the boards, as well as a couple of piles of everyday, fancy outdoor clothes that the Quality had left in to be cleaned and ironed.

Hetty pulled her filthy work dress over her head and reached for a clean Workhouse uniform as Matron had instructed, but Rose grabbed her arm. 'Hold your horses, Hetty,' she said, 'If we're getting out of here, we're getting out of here in style!' She grabbed four dresses from the clean and dried 'Quality' pile and handed them to Hetty and the two other girls. They quickly put them on, while the ironing inmates put down their hot irons and watched the girls with amusement. Billy and Shep stripped off their dresses and frilly caps too, revealing their more usual dress of shabby shirts and tatty trousers underneath. Billy was delighted to take his trusty, rusty old saucepan out of the cloth sack he had been carrying and put the battered pot back on his head where it belonged.

'Now I feel like Billy the Pan again,' he said happily. Then he turned to the women who were working at the huge, soapy vats. 'Pardon me, ladies,' he said, flashing them his best winning smile, 'are these hampers due to be collected any time soon.'

One woman lowered her wooden pole and smiled back, 'Meself and Maisie here are just about to bring them out to the gates – they're picked up around this time every Monday afternoon, but the lads who collect them are late.'

Billy winked at the two women, 'Well, we'll bring out a couple of them for you and save you a job!'

The line of laundry hampers stood beside the steaming vats and Billy dragged two of these over to the girls. 'In you go, ladies,' he said, 'two to each basket, if you please.' The girls smiled and cheerfully hopped into the baskets. Shep covered each pair of girls with a spare white sheet to hide them. 'Right, Shep,' he said, 'now that we are boys again, why don't we say that we are delivery boys, collecting these two baskets of clean dresses for the Quality?'

Shep grinned at his pal. 'An excellent idea, Mister the Pan; but let's not mention, if questioned, that each clean dress contains an escaping Workhouse inmate!' he said. 'No, we mustn't mention that!' agreed Billy the Pan. 'And ladies,' he said to the women working in the laundry, 'we'd be most grateful if you didn't mention anything about the contents of the dresses either!'

Billy and Shep dragged the two laundry hampers through the double doors, up the length of the Work-house work hall and out into the rainy courtyard. The Matron stood watching them, her arms folded over the chest of her brown uniform. She hadn't seen those two delivery boys before, but they seemed to know where they were going. She looked back to the doors of the laundry. *How long,* she thought, *does it take six girls to get changed?*

As soon as the children were through the orchard

and standing on the cobblestones at the other side of the Workhouse wall, the two girls from the table hugged Billy and Shep, waved to Hetty and Rose and disappeared down the road towards Thomas Street. Hetty and Rose brushed dust from their newly acquired dresses and stood back to admire each other's style. Suddenly there was a bark from the other side of the road and a brown, furry shape came across the cobbles like a rocket and launched itself into Hetty's arms.

'Prince Albert!' cried Hetty, 'You waited for me!' The dog was licking Hetty's chin and had such a big, delighted smile on its face that Rose, Billy and Shep couldn't help but laugh.

'So, what will you do now, Hetty?' asked Rose, when Hetty had put Prince Albert back on the ground and was wiping her dripping face, 'Will you go back to your gang?'

'I … I don't have a gang,' said Hetty, a little shame-facedly, 'I only pretended that I did. I've no gang and I've no family; it's always been just me. And Prince Albert, of course.'

'Well, Hetty,' said Billy, 'You have a gang now.'

'Yeah!' said Shep, grabbing her hand while Rose hugged Prince Albert, 'Welcome to The Sackville Street Spooks!'

CHAPTER TEN:

FULLY BOOKED

IN WHICH MOLLY, BRAM AND SANJIT VISIT THE LONG ROOM, AND
A FORGOTTEN TOMB, IN TRINITY COLLEGE

Bram woke to a loud, thunderous noise that sounded like someone throwing brim-full buckets of water against his bedroom windowpane. The watery clatter of hansom cabs and horse-drawn carriages sloshing through puddles could be heard from the cobblestoned street below. *Typical Monday morning – it always lashes at the start of the week when I*

171

have to go to school, Bram thought to himself sleepily, then remembered that it was the mid-term break (*No school!*) and that his friends Molly and Sanjit were staying over in the spare bedrooms. He leaped from his bed, poured cold water from a jug into the washbasin for a quick wash, brushed his teeth, got dressed and raced downstairs as a peal of thunder rang out from the saturated skies.

As he suspected, Molly and Sanjit were already up and were sitting at the breakfast table, eating boiled eggs and toast, listening cheerfully as Bram's mother chatted away to them. Her Majesty lay under the table, chewing on some pieces of fried bacon, her doggy eyes on the maid Lily, who was fussing around the dining room's fireplace.

'I've asked Lily to light the fire this morning, Bram, dear,' said his mother as she offered more toast to Sanjit, 'It's so dreadfully wet and cold out today. Molly tells me that you are planning a trip to the Library at Trinity College?'

Bram nodded as he sat down and helped himself to some bacon. 'You're not going this morning, I'm afraid,' said his mother, buttering a piece of toast,

'not in this dreadful downpour – I won't allow it!'
Bram started to protest, but just then another peal of
thunder sounded, this time loud enough to make the
breakfast room windows rattle in their frames. 'Yes,
Mama,' he said from behind his cup of tea, 'We shall
wait until the rain eases.'

Unfortunately, the rain did not ease all morning.
The children sat in the drawing room of 19 Buckingham Street, alternately leafing through books
from the bookshelves and looking at Captain Lamprey's map while they waited.

By eleven o'clock Molly was practically vibrat-
ing with impatience. 'How long is this rain going
to go on?' she asked nobody in particular, as she
glared out the window at the deluge of torrential
rain that was soaking the street. 'This isn't even real
rain! I mean, it's not good weather for bobbin', 'cause
there's nobody out on the streets – sorry, Sanjit, "bobbing" means pick-pocketin'; you know, robbin' rich
peoples' pockets. Rainy days were always our days off
– we used to go out and have great fun an' high jinks
in weather much worse than this!'

When Lily the maid called them in to lunch at

half past one, Molly was almost too frustrated to eat; but when she saw the dining room table laid out with large porcelain serving dishes covered in slices of ham and beef, baskets of fresh bread – with the crusts cut off – and two pots of steaming tea, she got over her frustration and graciously (and gratefully) sat down to eat. After years of living without a family, first in the Workhouse and then in the street, and even more years of looking out for her new family, the Spooks, Molly knew that hardship and hunger might never be more than one ham sandwich away. She never refused food, especially when it was offered freely and with kindness. Even when the bread had no crusts.

'You know, my dears,' said Bram's mother, as she drained her teacup and placed it delicately on its saucer, 'I think the storm may be abating.' Bram stood from the table and looked out the window – his mother was right; over lunch the thunder had died down and the rain had eased to a heavy drizzle.

'Now is our chance,' he said, turning to Molly and Sanjit. 'Mama, thank you for a lovely lunch.' Molly bounded to her feet, scraping her chair back. 'Yes,

Mrs Stoker,' she said in her plummiest voice, 'a most delectable meal!'

Bram's mama smiled; she liked this polite, mannerly, well-brought-up young girl. 'You are most welcome, my dear,' she said, 'and you and your young friend are welcome to stay here any time.' The children smiled back and nodded, and quickly made for the door.

'Oh! Be sure to wear your greatcoat and galoshes, Bram, just in case,' called his mother as the children bolted down the corridor, 'There are old ones downstairs that belong to your brother; poor Thornley – he's not back from England until his school breaks up for the summer, so he won't be needing them – they should fit Molly and Sanjit.'

Bram's father had taken the family's horse-drawn buggy to work at Dublin Castle that day, so Molly, Bram and Sanjit, kitted out in borrowed greatcoats and rubber galoshes covering their shoes, had to hail a cab for themselves on Buckingham Street. 'Trinity College, please, driver!' said Bram as they climbed up, glad to be out of the rain. Once inside, Her Majesty shook the rainwater off herself vigorously, to shouts from Bram and Sanjit, and delighted giggles from Molly.

None of the children noticed the tall, damp figure with water dripping from his long black beard that hailed another cab in the drenched street a few moments later and followed behind.

The white-stoned facade of Trinity College was picturesque and pretty despite the rain, and the polished oak door set into its arched portico was wide open. The buggy pulled up at the gate and the children hopped down and ran inside, trying, mostly unsuccessfully, to dodge the heavier of the raindrops. They strolled past the porters and one of them gave the children a courteous wave, which surprised Molly; she still wasn't used to being welcomed into fancy establishments as a member of the Quality (or at least the niece or ward of a member of the Quality) – she was much more used to being called a 'grubby-looking guttersnipe', being seen as a potential threat to peoples' property, and being summarily chased away. *It's amazing what a change of clothes and a fake-upper-crust accent can do for one's standing in polite society,* she thought, sending the porter an airy wave in return.

The children emerged from the other side of the stone arch and stood in its meagre shelter, gazing at the imposing, important-looking stone buildings that lay before them.

'That's the medical building, where the student doctors train,' explained Sanjit, pointing to a huge stone building on the left. 'That small arch in the middle of the square is a bell tower called the Campanile; that's the English Literature and History Studies building over there; and that ...' he pointed to a long building on the right, '... is the Library.'

Bram gazed around the campus at the beautiful buildings and imagined all the students inside, listening to interesting lectures, reading riveting books and learning fact after fascinating fact. He made up his mind there and then that he would one day join the ranks of those students – he would work hard and do the best he could at the boring Reverend Woods' dull and dreary school; then he would make it his business to attend Trinity College!

The Library was at the other side of a wide cobblestoned square and the children trotted across it as quickly as they could manage, bundling up in their borrowed greatcoats and being careful not to slip on the wet cobbles. Her Majesty scampered along behind them, barking gleefully.

'She will have to wait here,' said Sanjit when they reached the door of the Library. 'Sorry, Her Majesty, they don't allow dogs into the Long Room.' Her Majesty didn't seem too bothered about that, though; she gave a good-humoured yap and lay down to wait on the wet stone ground beside the Library door – she was a street dog after all, and she never let a little dampness bother her.

Molly gasped as they entered the Long Room. Its vaulted ceiling, high above them, was made of arched, polished oak beams, and looked like the inside hull of a wooden sailing ship. Holding up this immense ceiling were a series of magnificent carved oak columns, and at the end of each of these pillars were wooden pedestals. On each pedestal stood a white marble bust, depicting the head and shoulders of Greek philosophers such as Aristotle and Plato, playwrights and poets such as Shakespeare and Milton, and Irish literary figures like Jonathan Swift and

Oliver Goldsmith. But what dumbfounded Molly the most was the number of books the large room held; they seemed to have every book ever printed in Ireland, perhaps in the whole United Kingdom or maybe the entire world, out on display. Rows upon rows of books stood on rows upon rows of shelves and bookcases that jutted out from the side walls at right angles down the length of the ground floor of this long – and perfectly named – Long Room. In some of the large alcoves created by these towering bookcases, smaller bookcases stood, lit by tall windows and jam-packed with more books. In others, there were reading desks, with oil lamps and candlesticks for evening and night reading. Ladders with castor-wheels on their legs reached up to the higher levels of each neatly crammed bookcase, and librarians were climbing some of these, plucking the book-shaped fruit from the topmost shelves.

Above these lofty bookcases was yet another floor of shelves and cases, each holding the same number of books as the floor below. Bram glanced at Molly, noticing the look of wonder on her freckly face. 'There is so much to read here,' he whispered to his friend, 'but I bet *they* don't have a copy of *A Christmas Carol*, signed by Charles Dickens himself!' Then, looking at the huge quantity of books, Bram decided that they simply *must* have at least five signed copies *somewhere* around here. He also decided that he would most *definitely* like to attend Trinity College when he got older!

They shrugged off their wet greatcoats, hanging them on a coat rack, and left their soggy galoshes in a wicker basket beside the door. As she took off her coat, Molly took Captain Lamprey's folded map out of the pocket and held it up to the light. 'LONG ROOM,' she read aloud, 'NCC 1701D.' She looked at the tall bookcases that ran the length of the chamber; each had letters of the alphabet running down the side, one letter at the start of each shelf. 'That must mean the books are put on the shelves in alphabetical order,' she said to the boys, 'The map mentions the letters N, C and D … Bram, you look at all the shelves marked with N; Sanjit, you look at all the shelves marked D. I will check out all the C shelves.'

'What are we looking for?' asked Sanjit.

'I don't know, the map doesn't say,' said Molly,

squinting at the tiny writing on the old piece of parchment, 'Maybe look for a pirate book, maybe even a book about Captain Lamprey himself. I'm guessing that we will know what we are lookin' for when we find it!' They split up and started examining the books on the many lettered shelves to their left and right. The highest shelf on each bookcase was marked N, and Bram had to slide over the wheeled ladders to be able to see the books up there. *Just my luck,* he thought, wobbling up the ladder steps, *I'm not very good with heights.*

After an hour, they met again in the centre of the room where all three flopped down wearily on a wooden bench. 'Any luck?' asked Molly. 'None at all, I'm afraid,' replied Sanjit, 'I found the old book about Captain Lamprey that I was reading before, but when I looked at the first page of that I could see it was written in 1834 – Captain Lamprey couldn't have left a clue in there, 1834 was way after his time! I couldn't find any other books at all that looked suspicious.'

Bram shook his head, 'Me neither,' he said, 'There are books here about every subject under the sun, but I only found one book about pirates – that was written well after the Captain's time too.'

'I couldn't find anything either,' said Molly dejectedly. She gazed at the old piece of paper again, hoping that an idea, any idea, would jump off the page and present itself.

'My uncle used to bring me here before he was kidnapped,' said Sanjit, 'Whenever I asked him a question he'd call me a brat and hiss at me to be quiet; he'd tell me if I wanted to know anything, I'd have to ask the librarian.'

'That's it!' said Molly, standing up, 'We ask a librarian! They might know what the strange letters and numbers stand for.'

Molly marched over to the librarian's desk at the far end of the long room. She rapped her knuckles on the wooden top of the desk to get the librarian's attention and said, in the best fake upper-class accent she could muster, 'Excuse me, my good Miss Librarian madam, but would you by any chance know what the letters NCC 1701D might stand for?

The grey-haired librarian pushed her silver-rimmed spectacles back up onto the bridge of her nose and looked up at the children with kindly eyes, 'Oh, my dear, it's so nice to see children taking an interest in books!' She tapped a finger on her lips for a moment, deep in thought. 'NCC 1701D ...' she repeated quietly to herself, 'Oh! I think the NCC part may stand for "New Collection Catalogue"; that's not really a "new" collection, by the way, those books were part of the Cobb Bequest, given to the Library when Doctor Cobb died in 1801. It's just called "New" because it was "new" to us at the time.'

'Doctor Cobb!' whispered Sanjit, 'He's the man that Captain Lamprey gave the stuffed animals to!' The children looked at each other in wonder; Captain Lamprey had disappeared with the Rajapur Ruby a hundred years ago, and left his animals in the care of the very same man who left his book collection to the Trinity Library – could there be a book in Cobb's collection that would have a clue to where the pirate Captain had disappeared to?

'The 1701D is probably the catalogue number of an actual book in that collection,' continued the librarian, 'but you wouldn't find that book out on the shelves; the Cobb Bequest is held in storage, in the basement of the Library. Would you like me to see if I can find it for you?' The children nodded eagerly. The librarian stood up from the desk and wrote down the number on a page from her note-pad. 'Give me a few moments, my dears,' she said, 'and we'll see if we can find your book!' She disappeared down a wrought iron spiral staircase behind the desk.

After what seemed like a lifetime of waiting, the Librarian's grey head appeared again through the wooden floor as it, followed by the rest of her, ascended the staircase into the Long Room. The children were delighted to see that she was carrying a book in her wrinkled hands. 'Now, my dears,' she said, puffing and panting with the effort of the climb, 'I found your book! It's called *Aquatic Animales of the Deepe Sea* by J. L. Picard; it looks like an old book about animal life in the oceans.' She handed the book across the desk to Molly, who turned it over, examining the faded, red, cloth-bound book with its fancy gold foil lettering. 'Thank you so much, madam librarian, ma'am; I think this might be exactly what we are looking for!' she chirped, and the three friends hurried back to the wooden bench.

The date on the front page of the book gave the book's publication date as 1760. 'Just after Captain Lamprey's vanishing act!' said Bram excitedly. They looked though the book, flicking through the brittle paper pages, but could not see anything at first glance that might be a clue. Molly, with a quick look around at the Librarian's desk, held the book by its spine and shook it, hoping against hope that a concealed piece of paper might dislodge itself and flutter to the floor, but there were no clue-filled pages hidden within.

Bram ran his finger down the contents list at the start of the book. The chapter headings were written in very small letters, and in the rainy grey light that suffused the Long Room, he could just about make out the words. 'Chapter One: Seales of the Hebrides,' he read, 'Chapter Two is all about sponges; Three is starfish; then dolphins, whales, tuna fish, lamprey eels, haddock —'

Molly held up her hand, 'Hold on,' she said with urgency, 'Go back; did you say "lamprey eels"?'

Bram slid his finger back up the list. 'Yes!' he cried,

'Lamprey eels! Like Captain Lamprey! Chapter Seven, page 128!'

Bram flicked through the book to page 128.

'Here we are,' said Molly, 'Lamprey eels.' She squinted at the small type. '*The Lamprey*,' read Molly, '*is an ancient lineage of jawe-less fishe that are characterised by a tooth-less, sucking mouth which it uses to bore into other fishe and suck up of their bloode.*'

'Bloodsuckers!' said Bram, 'The lamprey is like a vampire fish!' He shuddered, his mother had been telling him stories about vampires since he was a little boy, and the thought of those white-faced, black-cloaked demons never failed to give him the creeps.

'There's nothing about Captain Lamprey in here though,' said Molly with a disappointed sigh, 'it's all about vampire eels.'

'Let me see,' said Sanjit, taking the red-covered book from Molly. He stood up from the bench and walked over to an alcove, where a tall window was casting grey light across the bookshelves. 'Here!' he exclaimed, 'Some of the words are underlined! I can just about make out the grey pencil lines!' Molly and Bram ran over and peered at the pages. Sanjit was right: some random words were underlined in faint grey.

'Well spotted, Sanjit,' said Bram, taking a notepad and pencil out of the pocket of his greatcoat. He licked the tip of the pencil and stood with it poised over the notepad, 'You've the best eyes, read out the words that are underlined and I'll write them down here.'

'Alright,' said Sanjit, screwing up his eyes and peering carefully at the page in the lamprey chapter, 'The first word underlined is *second*, as in *The lamprey eel is the second most dangerous* …; second word is *case*; the third is *from*; the next is *entrance*.'

He turned the page. 'Then there's *bottom* – as in *bottom of the sea*, not as in the bottom you sit on!', Sanjit giggled. 'The next word is *left* and then, ummmm, *side*.' He turned to the next page, 'On this page it's *passage* and *below*.' He scanned the next page, 'Nothing on this one, and that's the last page in the chapter; that must be it.'

Bram cleared his throat and read out the words he had written down in his notepad, 'A-hem. *Second case from entrance, bottom left side, passage below*.' He looked up at his two friends and smiled, 'What a clever way to leave a message,' he said, 'I wonder what it means?'

'Exactly what it says!' said Molly, grabbing the notepad from Bram and walking briskly to the Library door. '*Second case from entrance*,' she said, counting down two bookcases from the door, '*bottom left side* …' The three children examined the books on the left side of the bottom shelf of the bookcase.

'Nothing,' said Sanjit, 'No pirate books here.'

'*Passage below* …' said Bram slowly. He got down on his hands and knees and inspected the wooden floor. Was it his imagination, or could he feel a very slight draught of cold air rising up from the cracks between the straight, polished wooden floorboards that lay tight and flush beside each other? He licked his finger and held it over one of the cracks; he *could* feel a draught! 'Passage below!' he said excitedly. He felt around the sides of the wooden slat with his fingers, then, using his fingernails, he started to prise up one of the floorboards.

To Bram's astonishment, a square section of the wooden floor began to lift up, just like a trapdoor. It gave a high-pitched KREEEEEEAAAAAKKKK as it unfastened – it probably hadn't been opened in close to a hundred years – and Molly started to cough loudly, in a barking cough as fake as her wonky well-heeled accent, to mask the noise from listening librarians. Bram and Sanjit began to cough for a different reason: a cloud of stale dust was rising up from the pitch-black darkness revealed by the newly opened breach in the wooden floor. Bram leaned over and looked into the murky void. Seeing nothing in the blackness, he delved his arm in, feeling around the sides until his fingers felt rusty metal, a metal bar! 'I think there's a ladder here, I think I can feel the top rung,' he said, swinging his legs around into the hole, 'Let's see what's down in this tunnel that Captain Lamprey so wants us to explore!' He climbed down the ladder into the darkness below. Sanjit and Molly followed, but not before Molly grabbed one of the oil lamps from the alcove's reading table and lit it. *You can't explore what you can't see!* She handed the lamp down to Sanjit and, as she climbed into the hole, she pulled the disguised wooden door behind her. It closed again with a soft WHUMPFF, and the library alcove was once more empty, as if the children had never been there at all.

* * *

They climbed down a short metal ladder and found themselves in a tunnel, with solid walls of packed earth, supported by rough wooden beams.

'It looks like the inside of a mine,' said Sanjit.

'And a mine is where precious gemstones are discovered,' said Bram, smiling.

'Like rubies!' agreed Molly, 'C'mon, lads, let's find this Raja-whatsit Ruby! This way!'

Holding the oil lamp aloft, Molly led the way down the tunnel. The passage was surprising dry, given that morning's downpour. It was just about tall enough to stand up in, but the children walked with their backs slightly bent, not wanting to hit their heads. Every twenty steps or so they would come across a large, misshapen rock that had dislodged from the tunnel's ceiling and fallen onto the dirt floor. 'Move carefully,' said Molly, 'we don't want to cause a cave-in!'

A couple of minutes later and a little further down the tunnel, that was exactly what they found: a cave-in. A huge mass of soil, rocks and debris had fallen from the ceiling of the passage and was completely blocking their way. Molly held the oil lamp up to the blockage – there didn't seem to be any way through – but she had come this far, and she wasn't going to let a little thing like a blocked tunnel stop her now.

'C'mon lads,' she said, putting down her lamp, 'Use your hands like shovels – throw back your ears and dig!' Starting at the top of the tunnel, the children set about shifting the soil and debris, helping each other to move the bigger rocks, until there was a big enough space for them to crawl through one at a time.

'Ladies first!' said Molly, handing the oil lamp to Sanjit and wriggling through the gap in the blockage.

'Go gently,' advised Bram, 'There's already been a cave-in and we don't want another one – I don't think this tunnel is too stable!'

Once Molly was through, Sanjit reached into the gap and handed her the lamp.

'JANEY MACK!' cried Molly from the other side, 'Lads, wait 'til you see this!' The two boys scurried through the opening as fast as they could, knocking down clumps of dirt as they went. Sanjit and Bram clambered down the other side of the gap and came to a complete, astonished stop when they saw with their own eyes what Molly had been looking at.

Sitting upright up against one of the dirt walls, illuminated by the flickering light of Molly's oil lamp, was a human skeleton. The skeleton was wearing a long, tattered jacket, covered in cobwebs. It was made of a velvet fabric that may have once been red, and had two lines of silver buttons hanging off by thin threads on both sides. On the skeleton's feet were two rotten leather boots, and a rusty cutlass sword and a dusty black pirate hat lay on the dirt ground beside him. His white, bony skull had two empty, black eye sockets and a full mouth of grinning white teeth. The skull had an ominous, ragged-edged hole in the top, as if the bone had been bashed in by a rock.

'Captain Lamprey?' cried Bram, his hand involuntarily travelling to his mouth in shock.

'It's got to be!' said Molly, bringing the lamp nearer to the skeleton's face for a closer look. The bony face seemed to grin back at her. 'So *this* is where you disappeared to!'

'Look at the skull,' said Bram, 'it looks like the same cave-in that we clambered through may have caved in his poor head!' Molly grimaced, 'What a way to go …'

'But look what's in his hand,' exclaimed Sanjit, 'a treasure chest!' Clutched in Captain Lamprey's bony fingers was a small wooden box with a domed lid that certainly looked very much like a pirate's treasure chest from an illustrated children's book, but just much smaller.

'That box is too small to hold any treasure,' said Molly, 'it would only just about hold an apple.'

'Or maybe a cannonball,' agreed Sanjit.

'Or … the Rajapur Ruby!' shouted Bram. He bent down and carefully removed the tiny treasure chest from Captain Lamprey's skeletal fingers. Molly and Sanjit leant in as Bram opened the box … and then slumped in disappointment when Bram took out what was inside: not the Rajapur Ruby, but a small, leatherbound journal.

'Not another clue,' said Molly, 'C'mon Captain, what have you got for us this time?'

Bram opened the journal; it was full of yellowed, brittle pages, all of them as fragile as dried leaves – and all of them completely blank. Bram flicked though the pages delicately, feeling a gentle panic rise, until he reached the final two. He heaved a sigh of relief; these pages had handwriting scrawled across them.

Sanjit held the oil lamp while Bram read the words written on the pages – it seemed to be the same spidery handwriting as on the map they found inside the stuffed bear. '*The final steppe that ye must take,*' he read, '*Now that ye have founde my booke, Is to use the mappe where the dead lie a-sleeping, In the towne of Donnybrooke.* "Where the dead lie a-sleeping" – that must mean a graveyard, but the map we found definitely wasn't a map of Donnybrook.'

'He must have been planning to hide this treasure box down here in the tunnel,' said Molly, 'when the tunnel caved in and killed him.' She shook her head, 'Ah, the poor creature ...'

Suddenly there was a loud KERRASSHHHH!! behind them and the children were enveloped in a cloud of dust. Coughing, Sanjit held the lamp up to the opening they had come through; it was completely sealed shut again by a fall of earth and rocks from the tunnel ceiling above.

'We have to get out of here,' said Sanjit, 'I think

that this place is falling apart!'

'Well,' said Bram, 'we can't get back to the Library now, we will have to push on forward and hope that this tunnel leads somewhere.'

Molly took the piece of parchment they had just found and put it into the pocket she had sewn into folds of her dress. 'Oh Bram,' she said, 'Every tunnel leads somewhere – even those that lead to dead ends!'

They bid farewell to the skeleton of poor Captain Lamprey and walked slowly along the tunnel in the only direction they could. After a while Bram thought he could feel a breeze on his face, and soon after that Molly imagined she could hear trickling water. The darkness in the tunnel seemed to become less dense as they walked, and the air seemed to become less stale. The sound of dripping, dribbling water became stronger too, and the earth walls looked wet and slick in the oil lamp light.

A little further on the earth walls had become stone walls and the children reached a set of rough stone steps that spiralled upwards. With Molly lead-ing the way again, the children climbed the steps until they reached the dead end that she had predicted – a grey stone slab which lay across the top of the spiral staircase, sealing it closed. Molly, Bram and Sanjit raised their hands and pushed at the flat stone with all their might. At first it didn't move, but then it started to shift in place a little, causing dust and fragments of small stone and plaster to fall on their heads in a soft rain. With a sudden jerk, the stone slab slid across the opening and weak daylight flooded into the tunnel. Bram climbed out of the passage and reached down to help Molly and Sanjit up.

They found themselves in a stone chamber beside a craggy stone well, full almost to the brim with black water. More water babbled into the well from a crack in the rock wall above it.

'St Patrick's Well!' said Sanjit, delighted to be out of the cramped and dusty tunnel. 'This is the holy well at the side of the College at Nassau Street; it's hundreds of years old – it was here well before Trinity College itself. The tunnel must have come all the way from the Library to here!'

'It's not too far from Nassau Street to Donnybrook, and the graveyard in Donnybrook seems to be where the Captain wants us to go,' said Bram, 'We can try and hail a cab when we get out — if we *can* get out, that is.' He studied the sturdy wooden door that barred their exit from the stone well chamber. It proved to be locked tight — locked tight that is, until Molly took a hairpin from her bushy red hair and effortlessly picked the iron lock. 'Still the best sneak thief in Dublin!' she said with a wink as the door swung open.

They emerged into the grey afternoon light of Nassau Street. Cabs and carriages clanked noisily as they rolled in both directions up and down the busy street. The children's clothes were grimy with tunnel muck, with more dust and debris coated their hair. Although the rain had finally stopped, the three children shook themselves like wet dogs to dislodge the worst of the earth and soil. A happy bark in the distance announced the arrival of Her Majesty, who, catching their scent on the wind, bounded across the length of the campus and through the side gate of Trinity College to join the children. She bounced up and down beside them happily, trying to lick their dusty faces and hands.

Bram raised his hand to hail a cab, but to his puzzlement the driver studiously ignored him, and the carriage sailed past. It was the same story with the next carriage, and the next after that. 'It's our clothes!' exclaimed Molly, 'We are covered in muck from the tunnel, our clothes are filthy, and we look like street urchins!' Molly, who had some idea of what it was like to be judged – and condemned – on appearance alone, knew what to do. She raised both her little fingers to her mouth, took a deep breath and blew out three ear-splitting whistles – two high and one low. Sanjit, who hadn't heard Molly's signature whistle before, stuck his grimy fingers in his ears.

Three cabs immediately came to a stop in front of them. 'Look at that,' said Molly, swinging herself up into the first carriage, 'you wait for one cab, and then three turn up at the same time!' The boys climbed after her, with Her Majesty hopping up behind them, and the cab set off in the direction of Donnybrook.

None of the children noticed a tall man dislodging himself from a stone doorway on the opposite side of the street. The man raised a hand and a carriage stopped instantly. He boarded the carriage and, striking a match on the cab's ceiling, lit a cigar which he placed between his gleaming white teeth. 'Driver,' he snarled, his sly face wreathed in grey cigar smoke, 'follow that cab.'

Chapter Eleven:

A Very Grave Situation ...

IN WHICH THE SPOOKS VISIT A GRAVEYARD AND FACE DOWN
A BLOWHARD

When their cab turned onto Merrion Square, the children heard a shout from the side of the street. Looking out the carriage window they saw Billy the Pan and Shep waving at them, and Bram called to the driver to stop the cab. Molly was delighted to see that they had Rose with them, although she was somewhat less delighted to find Hetty Hardwicke *(of all people!)* with them too.

'Hetty's one of us now,' said Rose as she climbed onboard the carriage, 'We made friends in the Workhouse; isn't that right, Hetty?' Hetty, looking a little shamefaced, climbed aboard too, with Prince Albert in her arms. Her Majesty growled at Prince Albert, who put his head down and whimpered. Then Molly's dog sniffed Hetty's dog vigorously from head to tail, and gave him a lick on the snout.

'Well,' said Molly, 'if Her Majesty thinks you're both alright, then you must be; she's a very good judge of character!' With all The Sackville Street Spooks onboard, the carriage rolled on to Donnybrook.

On the way, Billy and Shep told the others about the jailbreak from the Workhouse, and Molly revealed the clues that had brought them to the Library, and what they had discovered in the tunnel underneath.

'So you found the actual, real life Captain Lamprey – well, the *dead* Captain Lamprey, with his poor head caved in – but there's still no sign of Sanjit's uncle?' asked Rose. She patted Sanjit on the knee, 'Poor pet.'

Donnybrook village was busy with carts, buggies

and children walking hand in hand with their parents, and the reason for all this activity soon became apparent to the children.

'The Big Top!' said Molly, pointing at Donnybrook Field where the huge red and white striped canvas tent of Mr Pablo Fanque's Circus Royal was standing tall, its flag fluttering in the wind and crowds of excited-looking people making their way past the sideshow tents and milling about the entrance. 'Wild Bert did say that the circus was on today at Donnybrook; we must call in and say hello after we've given this graveyard the once-over.'

The heavy iron gates to Donnybrook Cemetery creaked as Bram pushed them open. The Spooks walked under the heavy stone arch and into the graveyard with an anxious Sanjit trailing a little behind.

'C'mon, brudder,' said Shep, going back and throwing his arms over the nervous boy's shoulders, 'there's nuthin' to be scared of in here – this is the "dead" centre of Donnybrook!' Billy the Pan laughed, 'Yeah, people are "dying" to get in here!'

Both those jokes, as awful as they were, managed

to put a small smile on Sanjit's face, and he allowed his 'brudder' to lead him in.

The graveyard was small, and in an advanced state of neglect and disrepair. The headstones jutted out of the long grass like the broken teeth of an ancient witch. Here and there stone tombs that lay flat, surrounded by knee-high rusting fences, were being choked by thick-growing weeds. Creeping moss and lichen obscured the writing on most of them. Her Majesty sniffed at a few of the gravestones, while Prince Albert sniffed at Her Majesty.

Molly took out the parchment they had found in Captain Lamprey's tiny treasure chest. '*The final steppe that ye must take,*' she read, '*Now that ye have founde my booke, Is to use the mappe where the dead lie a-sleeping, In the towne of Donnybrooke ...*'

'Here we are *where the dead lie a-sleeping,*' said Bram, 'Mol, give me a look at Lamprey's map.' Molly handed Bram the first piece of paper they had found hidden inside the giant stuffed grizzly bear, and he squinted at the handwritten letter N and lines of block shapes beside it that covered the bottom half on one side of the page. The blocks didn't seem to correspond to streets or roads, certainly not to roads in Donnybrook. Donnybrook was well beyond the city, practically out in the countryside – Billy the Pan had complained on the carriage ride out that he didn't like to leave Dublin City, that he was born and bred between the confines of the Royal Canal and the Grand Canal and that was where he wanted to stay, thank you very much. There weren't enough roads here in Donnybrook to match the map; apart from the main road that led south towards Stillorgan, there were only one going east and a couple more going west. And there weren't enough buildings in the whole of Donnybrook village to match all the blocks printed on Lamprey's map either. *In fact,* thought Bram, *there are as many blocks on the map as there are graves in this cemetery …*

'Of course!' cried Bram, 'These blocks aren't buildings, these blocks on the map are graves!'

The Spooks crowded around the small map. 'And that letter N stands for north!' said Sanjit.

'Good thinkin', brudder,' said Shep, 'Now we know what way up the map is!'

'Which way is north?' asked Rose. 'Donnybrook

is south of the City,' said Molly, 'So north is back the way we came!' She pointed towards Dublin City and Bram turned the map around in his hands until the letter N was pointing in the direction of the city.

'Yes!' he cried, 'The blocks match the gravestones! This row of blocks matches this row here, and this row matches that one over there!'

'Well done, Quality,' said Molly, 'but it still doesn't tell us what we're looking for.'

'Can I have a look?' asked Hetty. Bram gave her the pirate map and she held it up close to her face. 'Now,' she said, pointing at the writing over the hand-drawn blocks, 'I can't read, so I don't know what any of these skinny words here say – they look like an ant stood in a paint pot and went for a walk – but did any of yiz notice that all of these blocks are drawn in black ink ... except for this one here?'

Molly grabbed the paper from her former rival and peered at it, 'Hetty! You're right! I could kiss you!' She pointed at a block in the middle of the second row from the bottom of the page, 'Bram, look – this block is in red ink!'

'Second row from the back of the cemetery, five

graves across! Let's go!' he said, already hurrying towards the graveyard's rear wall. When they got to the grave they found that it wasn't a grave at all; it was a fragment of an old wall, perhaps a broken wall from a demolished church that had stood here hundreds of years before. Halfway up the wall was a rectangular stone plaque, dedicated to a Doctor Bartholomew Cobb; under his name was written, 'Member of the Royal Dublin Society,' as well as his date of birth and date of death. Around the four edges of the stone was carved what seemed to be a poem.

'Doctor Cobb!' said Sanjit, 'Captain Lamprey's friend that he gave his stuffed animals to! This must be the last clue!'

Bram read out the carved inscription that ran around the plaque's perimeter.

> **'Follow in the Captain's steppes,**
>
> **To a mystery ye must yet unravel,**
>
> **If ye seeke the brightest starre,**
>
> **By Ursa Minor thee must travel.'**

'Not another poem!' said Molly with a sigh, 'Look,

it's getting late, and this graveyard is not somewhere I want to be after dark; Bram, write down what it says in your notebook and let's get out of here.'

They walked across the street to Donnybrook Field where they could hear the muted tones of a steam organ playing carnival music and muffled sounds of laughter; Pablo Fanque's circus was in full swing! The children passed around the notebook in the flickering firelight of a torch attached to a pole that stood by the row of sideshow tents; there were no gas lamps on the streets of Donnybrook, it was much too far outside the city.

'I suppose the "starre" is the Rajapur Ruby?' said Molly, passing the notebook to Hetty. Hetty, not being able to read, wrinkled her nose at the pages and passed it on to Billy straight away.

'Yes,' said Bram, 'but sailors navigate using the stars; they can tell where north, south, east and west are by the position of the constellations – you know, sets of stars in the sky that look like things – there are three stars that form Orion's Belt, there's another constellation called Taurus because it looks like a bull. *Ursa Minor* is a constellation too. Americans call *Ursa*

Minor the Little Dipper because the stars in it form a shape like a spoon.'

'Bram,' said Sanjit slowly, 'Isn't "*Ursa*" Latin for the word 'bear'?'

'Oh. My. Dog.' said Molly, making Her Majesty raise her head and give her a quizzical look, *If ye seeke the brightest starre, By Ursa Minor thee must travel* – *Ursa Minor* means the little bear! There are two bears in the Dead Zoo – one big –'

'And one little!' said Bram, '*Ursa Minor*! The ruby is in the Little Bear! We've got to get back to the Museum right now!'

'Of course!' said a deep voice from behind the children, 'What a fool I've been – the ruby is hidden in the little bear – the one animal I didn't slice open!'

They turned to see a tall man with a long black beard. His clothes were damp and bedraggled, but his eyes, set beneath bristling black eyebrows, sparkled with malice and greed.

'Uncle Seth!' exclaimed Sanjit. 'What do you mean?' Sanjit's mouth fell open and the colour drained out of his face, 'Did – OH! Were you looking for the ruby all along?!'

The tall man replied with a vicious, cackling laugh. 'Idiot children!' he sneered. 'You've solved this puzzle for me — you've told me where the Rajapur Ruby is hidden, and now ... I am going to get it!' Her Majesty and Prince Albert began to growl and bark; they could tell that this man was up to no good.

With a scornful laugh at the two dogs, the tall man leapt into the driver's seat of a big red wagon that was parked beside the Big Top. He gave the wagon's horse a sharp crack with the whip. The horse gave a surprised NEEEEIGGGHHH! and the carriage took off like a flying cannonball across the grass and rocketed away up the dust road towards the city.

'UNCLE SETH!' cried Sanjit in disappointment, coughing in the cloud of dust left by the fleeing wagon. So, Seth wasn't kidnapped after all? Sanjit couldn't believe his own uncle could be so cunning, not to mention so evil!

'We have to get to the Museum before he does!' shouted Bram. He looked around fruitlessly for another form of transport; there were a couple more wagons standing around, but none of them had horses hitched to them. They were stuck!

The side flap of the Big Top swung open and thunderous applause filled the air as a troupe of animals – a tall antlered stag, an African antelope, a black and white-striped zebra and a tiny Shetland pony – proudly trotted out, each wearing a leather, rhinestone-encrusted saddle. These were followed by a huge white horse, on top of which sat a man wearing a snow-white, equally rhinestone-encrusted suit. His head was covered by a huge white hat with a long blue feather in the brim and his elaborately curled, grey moustache gleamed in the bright lights from the circus ring.

'WILD BERT!!' shouted Molly, her face lighting up brighter than the circus spotlights.

'Well, yee-haw, little lady,' said Bert, 'I hope you guys ain't lookin' for tickets, because I've just finished my act!'

'We need to get to the Natural History Museum!' said Bram, 'As quick as we can! Uncle Seth has found out where the Raja–'

'Woah! Hold your hosses there, Bram!' said Wild Bert, 'If you need to get someplace in a hurry, why, I got your means of transport right here, all trained up and fast as the devil himself! Hop onboard my menagerie of animals!' He took out some carrots from holders on his belt and handed them to the animals who crunched them down greedily. 'Shucks,' he said, 'these guys will do anything for a carrot!'

The children climbed onto the animals' backs – Billy and Hetty on the stag; Shep and Sanjit got onto the antelope; and Molly and Bram on the zebra. All of them looked a little unsure as the animals whinnied, grunted and neighed happily under their weight.

Here we go, though Bram, wobbling slightly as he clung onto Molly's waist on the back of their black and white-striped steed, *Riding on the Menagerie, just like good old Captain Lamprey!*

Wild Bert leant down and pulled Rose up behind him onto the back of Buttercup. 'To the Museum!' he cried, 'Hi-yo, Buttercup! Away!' The mounted menagerie set off at a gallop, with Her Majesty and Prince Albert running and barking beside them.

As the strange collection of animals took off towards Dublin City with the children clinging to their backs, a brightly-coloured figure came out of a flap at the side of Pablo Fanque's Big Top.

'Hey,' said Bump-o the clown to the tiny Shetland pony as he looked at the large empty space beside the tent, 'Who took my trick wagon?'

CHAPTER TWELVE:

ANIMAL CRACKERS

IN WHICH MOLLY AND BRAM TRACK DOWN A TREASURE AND
RESCUE A RELATIVE

'AAAAGGGHHHHHHH!' screamed Bram, holding the reins tight as the zebra he and Molly were clinging to barrelled along Upper Leeson Street at full speed. Molly, using all the riding skills she had learned from her American friend Little Feather, was guiding the zebra by his brushy mane and whispering soothing words into his ears as they galloped.

The other children were careening behind them on their mounts, all whooping with excitement and exhilaration, and Wild Bert and Rose were a little ahead of them on Buttercup, leading the stampede.

Ahead of Buttercup was the red wagon, being driven at a mad pace by the equally mad tall man. He raised the whip again and again, bringing it snapping down cruelly on the poor horse's backside. As the wagon went over the hump of Leeson Street Bridge, something unexpected happened; there was a loud crack and the sound of a tooty, hooty, circus-clown horn and one of the wagon's wooden wheels shot off sideways. The wagon lurched to the left and the tall man held on to the side to keep his seat. Then, with another hooty horn sound and a wrenching noise, the wheel on the opposite side of the wagon shot off too. The tall man dropped his whip and clung on to the back of his seat with two hands. The wagon righted itself and the man thought he might just about be able to stay onboard, but the seat he was clinging to had other ideas; it abruptly shot up into the air, powered by a massive, coiled metal spring, taking the tall man with it. For a few long seconds the man flew through the air in a curved arc, his hands still on the red wooden seat; and then he began to fall. There was a huge SPLASSSHHH! as he landed in the deep water of the Grand Canal beside the bridge. Several ducks flapped up from the water and away, quacking angrily. The man bobbed to the surface a few seconds later, his long beard and curly ended moustache covered in canal weed and duck poo. The wrecked wagon's panting horse looked over the edge of the bridge and gave a laugh-like whinny.

The children cheered and raced past on their galloping menagerie.

'I think he's split his kipper, Mol!' shouted Billy the Pan, one foot coming free of the stirrups as he held on for dear life to the antlers of his stag. The animals kept galloping, turning right at Fitzwilliam Street and then left at Merrion Square, and reaching the Natural History Museum in mere seconds.

The Museum was locked up for the night and its windows were dark, but Sanjit jumped from his antelope's saddle and ran across the lawn to the side door, opening it with his key. 'Quickly! Bring the animals in,' he said, 'Uncle Seth might still have his whip and I don't want them to be harmed!'The children led the menagerie through the door and into the Museum, followed by Wild Bert and Buttercup.

The Museum, bright and airy during daytime, looked very different in the evening light.The assembled stuffed and skeletal animals looked slightly sinister, and their frames threw menacing shadows across the red-and-black diamonds of the tiled Museum floor.

Bram and Molly went straight to the display that held Captain Lamprey's stuffed *Menagerie* crew. The Museum staff had made some effort to tidy up the display and put the animals back together, but even so they stood at woozy, awkward poses and their fur had been re-stitched in quite a slipshod and slapdash way. The broken glass had been removed and Molly stepped up onto the display case as soon as she reached it.

Ignoring the other animals, she picked up the small bear. She could feel the gaze of the crocked crocodile, the wonky wolf, the messed-up moose and most of all the banjaxed mama bear as she brought the tiny stuffed bear cub, untouched and perfect, out of the display.

The other, real-life menagerie, Wild Bert's zebra, antelope and stag, whinnied and neighed until Bert calmed them down. 'Still, fellers,' he said in a soothing tone, 'I want y'all to stand as still as these stuffed animals – I think Mol's about to attempt what ya might call a tricky procedure.' Bram turned up the nearest gas lamps and they laid the furry object on the red-and-black tiled floor. The children and Wild Bert crowded around Bram and Molly, like student doctors at Trinity College about to watch an operation.

'Well, *Ursa Minor*,' said Molly, 'let's see what secrets you have been keeping all these years.' She turned the small bear over, and with her small fingernails delicately pulled at the threads at the base of the bear cub's neck. The stitching began to loosen and open up wider and wider as she worked. Soon the stitching was open down the line of the spine and, very gently, Molly started to pull the fur apart to reveal light yellow stuffing inside.

Bram watched as she pulled out the stuffing bit by fluffy bit, until a paper-wrapped shape revealed itself.

'Not more paper,' whispered Bram. Molly pulled out the shape slowly.

'It's heavy, whatever it is,' she said, and began to unwrap the object.

Even in the dim gas light the stone that was uncovered by Molly's trembling hand sparkled and glimmered more strongly than anything any of them had seen before. It was bright red, *ruby red*, and was ingeniously cut into the shape of a heart. It was the size of Molly's fist, maybe even as big as Wild Bert's cowboy fist, and its many facets glinted and shone with red light.

'The Rajapur Ruby ...' said Sanjit in wonder.

'And it's mine!' said a deep voice that boomed in the tall Museum chamber, bouncing off the ceiling and echoing off the walls, 'The ruby is mine! MINE!! Give it to me!'

The tall man stood on the tiled floor, his clothes wet and dripping, with canal weeds hanging soggily from his beard. One hand was outstretched; in his other he carried a knife, its blade long and sharp. It looked deadly, despite the duck poo that clung to it.

'No, Uncle Seth, you can't have it!' exclaimed
Sanjit, 'This Ruby once belonged to the Sultan of
Rajapur – it belongs to India now!'

'I AM NOT YOUR UNCLE!' screamed the tall
man, 'You idiot child! I don't even *have* any brothers
or sisters!'

'Oh,' said Hetty, 'I used to think that too, and then
I met The Sackville Street Spoo–'

'SHUT UP!!' roared the man, 'You are ALL idiot
children! I kidnapped your uncle *weeks* ago – I have
him tied up downstairs!' His face had turned red
as the ruby in Molly's hands, and white spittle was
seeping from the edges of his snarling lips. 'I have
posed as his double for weeks, taking care of this
idiot child! Now, give me the Ruby, or your precious uncle will get … this!' He held up the knife;
the razor-sharp blade flashed and glinted. Nobody
moved.

'On second thoughts,' he said, 'this idiot child is
closer to me than your uncle!' Fast as a viper he
reached out and grabbed Shep, snatching the small
boy to him and holding him tight in a vice-like grip.

He moved the blade menacingly towards Shep's face. Rose gave a little high-pitched squeal of fright, and the boy's eyes grew wide with terror.

Wild Bert's hand immediately twitched towards the holster on his belt. 'Don't bother going for your six-gun, *Cowboy*,' sneered the tall man, 'I know all you idiot circus rodeo riders never have real bullets, only blanks.'

'Who said I was going for ma gun?' asked Wild Bill. He pulled two carrots, long, orange and juicy, from his belt holsters and held them up to his menagerie, 'Go get 'im, boys!'

They had been standing as still as statues – as still as stuffed animals – but at the sight of the carrots, the stag, the zebra, the antelope, and even Butter-cup herself reared up on their hind legs. The tall man, shocked, stumbled backwards with a strangled scream. He dropped both the knife and Shep, and covered his eyes with his hands, screaming with fear and fright. 'Lamprey's stuffed animals!' he shrieked, 'They are ALIVE!'

'They're alive, alright!' said Bram, 'Alive, alive, oh!'

As one, the children dived onto the tall man, sitting

on his chest and holding him by the long beard. Her Majesty and Prince Albert stood over him, growling and baring their teeth as he whimpered in disappointment and defeat.

'You keep on calling us idiot children,' said Molly, holding up the ruby so the man could see it clearly; it sparkled and shone, 'but who's the eejit now? Bram, as much as I hate to say these words, I think it might be time to call the police.'

'Sanjit?' said a weak voice from a doorway behind them. Sanjit, who was sitting on the tall man's legs, turned to find Billy the Pan standing at the top of the basement steps, supporting a man with dark skin and a long black beard. The man was barefoot and wore filthy, stained clothes; he rubbed at red marks on his recently-freed wrists and looked at the boy with a familiar shy smile.

'UNCLE SETH!' cried Sanjit and ran into his *real* uncle's arms.

Bram looked down at the tall man who lay on the Museum floor, pinned down by Spooks, then he looked at Sanjit's real uncle, who was hugging the boy and crying. 'You know,' he said to Molly as she tossed the heart-shaped Rajapur Ruby from palm to palm, 'They really do look alike – Sanjit's uncle and the tall fellow here. They could almost be twins.'

Molly wrinkled her ginger eyebrows and gave Bram a sceptical stare. 'They are both lanky and they both have beards,' she said, 'but only an absolute eejit would think they were the same person.'

Bram put his finger to his lips. 'Shhhh, Mol,' he whispered, 'he fooled poor Sanjit into thinking he was his uncle, not to mention everybody here at the Museum. Let's just agree with them that they look like doubles.'

'Hmmmm … *Double Trouble at the Dead Zoo*,' said Molly with a wink, 'I think I like the sound of that.'

Bram grinned and winked back at his best friend, 'The Dead Zoo? I keep telling you, Molly – that name will never catch on!'

ME JEWEL AN' DARLIN' DUBLIN

As quiet as mice – mice who had a bad case of laryngitis as well as woolly socks and slippers on their tiny paws – Bram and Molly started to creep up the stairs to the top floor of Dublin Castle's Tavistock Tower.

Bram put his fingers to his lips as they passed the door to his father's office, but he needn't have worried about disturbing his dad – Papa Stoker was leaning back in his padded leather office chair, his spectacles off and his eyes closed, taking time out for an 'executive nap'. Molly listened to the soft snores coming from behind the closed door and shifted the carpet bag she was carrying from one hand to the other. They resumed climbing the stairs.

The two friends reached the very top of the Tower and crossed the landing to the locked strongroom door. Bram raised his eyebrows and Molly nodded. She took a hairpin from her red, bushy hair and set to work. In seconds she had picked all four locks and they were standing before the strongroom safe.

The safe was made of grey-green metal, was brand new, and looked formidable. A huge ivory-coloured circular combination lock dial was positioned dead centre of the heavy safe door. Molly nodded to Bram, *Your turn*. He got onto his knees and turned the dial to the numbers eight, eleven, then eighteen and forty-seven; the date of his birthday, the eighth of November, Eighteen Forty-seven – with any luck, his father would have kept the same combination that he had used for the last safe.

He had; the safe door clicked twice and swung open.

Molly reached into the safe and took out the box that contained the fake Irish Crown Jewels. She swapped them for the real ones from her carpet bag, then she put the box back and closed the safe. The two children left the strongroom and went silently down the stairs.

The sky was dark blue and full of twinkling stars as the friends walked out of the Tavistock Tower, closing the tall wooden door behind them. It locked itself with a soft click.

'Done and dusted,' said Molly, slapping her hands together, 'The Irish Crown Jewels are back where they belong – just like me.'

'That's two sets of jewels we have returned to their rightful place so,' said Bram, 'the Irish Crown Jewels are finally back safe and sound in Dublin Castle, that tall fella with the beard is safe and sound too, in prison, and Sanjit and his Uncle are taking the Rajapur Ruby back to Bombay – soon the ruby will be back where *it* belongs too!'

A huge, snow-white full moon hung over Dublin Castle, making the courtyard cobblestones glint and gleam with its silvery light. A little black bat flew across its perfectly round face with flappy, jerky wings. Molly took the carpet bag she was carrying and chucked it into a nearby bin; it landed at the bottom with a clunk, the fake Irish Crown Jewels inside jingling quietly.

'This, Bram,' said Molly with a small shiver, 'would be a perfect night for those monster yokes you are trying to write that story about; the blood suckers – what are they called?'

'Vampires,' said Bram.

'Vampires, that's right,' said Molly, 'Oh! I came up with a good name for the bad guy in your story: he's bad, he likes blood, so how about Count Badblood? Or, if you want to be all fancy about it, "bad blood" in Irish is something like "*droch fola*".'

'Count *Droch Fola*,' mused Bram, 'Hmmm. Or maybe just "Dracula" to make it snappier?'

Molly and Bram linked their arms together and walked across the moonlit Castle cobblestones.

'Count Dracula' said Molly, 'I like it, Bram. I think Dracula's a name that might actually catch on ...'

Author's note on Dublin:

Many of the Dublin locations in this book are as real as can be and can be visited today. Bram's home at **19 Buckingham Street** still stands; there is even a plaque to announce that he lived there, as well as a painting of his most famous character, Dracula, on the wall. **College Green**, where Billy and Shep encounter Hetty Hardwicke, still stands before **Trinity College**. The college itself is as beautiful today as it was in 1859, and the **Library Long Room** remains one of the most impressive and awe-inspiring places to visit in the world. **St Patrick's Well** can be tricky to find, but is still nestled at the side wall of the College at Nassau Street. The **South Dublin Workhouse** is demolished now, but the wall of the main building still hulks menacingly over James Street. **Ringsend**, a short walk from the city, is where the Dublin shoemakers held their **Waxies' Dargle** picnics – there's even a tavern there called The Merry Cobbler! **Pablo Fanque** was a real person; his real name was William Darby, and he was the most famous Black circus owner in Britain. **Pablo Fanque's Circus Royal** was a real circus too, and toured extensively around Britain and Ireland in the mid-1800s. **Donnybrook Cemetery** is situated beside the Garda Station in Donnybrook; the old church wall with its grey stone plaque still stands amongst the headstones. **Donnybrook Field**, where the Circus Royal held its second performance in the book, and where, in real life, the infamous Donnybrook Fair used to be held, is now a shiny, modern rugby stadium. The park at **Merrion Square** is a public park now, and is a lovely, green space to take time out from the hustle and bustle of city life. Young **Oscar Wilde**'s childhood home stands at No. 1 Merrion Square – there's even a laid-back statue to the famous playwright in the park! And lastly, of course, the **Natural History Museum** – or the **Dead Zoo**, as Molly would have it – still stands beside Leinster House on Merrion Square, but you won't find Captain Lamprey's menagerie of animals there; the bears, the moose, the wolf, the mountain lion and even the one-armed crocodile are all works of fiction. The Dead Zoo has been refurbished and repaired over the years, and with its stuffed animals, interesting exhibits and towering skeleton elks, it remains an amazing place to spend an afternoon.

Why not visit some of these places the next time you're in Dublin city? They might even inspire you, just like Bram, to become a writer!

AUTHOR'S NOTE ON INDIA

In 1858 India, like Ireland, was part of the far-reaching British Empire. The modern-day cities of Mumbai and Kolkata were known then, by British and Indian people alike, by their anglicised names, Bombay and Calcutta. In 1859 the only way to travel from India to Ireland was by sailing ship – it was a long journey, but it gave people plenty of time to read books!

The Real Bram & Molly

Bram Stoker

The *real* Bram Stoker was born and raised in Marino Crescent in Clontarf. After school he attended Trinity College in Dublin where was a star athlete. He always had a great love of writing and theatre, and after college he first became a newspaper theatre critic, and, after that, a theatre manager in London ... and then he decided to combined these two loves to write books such as *Dracula*, *The Lady in the Shroud*, and *The Lair of the White Worm*. His wife's name was Florence!

Molly Malone

Molly is *definitely* a fictional character, best known from the famous Dublin song where she roams the

City streets selling cockles and mussels, *'alive alive-oh!'*
She's a fishmonger in my book too, as well as a born
leader, an accomplished pickpocket and 'the best
sneak thief in Dublin'' But, to Bram, Molly is much
more than that – she's a true and faithful friend.

The Songs

Molly Malone

(*Traditional*)

In Dublin's fair city
Where the girls are so pretty
I first set my eyes on sweet Molly Malone
As she wheeled her wheelbarrow
Through streets broad and narrow
Crying, 'Cockles and mussels, alive, alive, oh!'

She was a fishmonger
And sure 'twas no wonder
For so were her father and mother before
And they both wheeled their barrows
Through streets broad and narrow
Crying, 'Cockles and mussels, alive, alive, oh!'

She died of a fever
And no one could save her
And that was the end of sweet Molly Malone
But her ghost wheels her barrow
Through streets broad and narrow
Crying, 'Cockles and mussels, alive, alive, oh!'

Alive, alive, oh
Alive, alive, oh
Crying 'Cockles and mussels, alive, alive, oh!'

Captain Lamprey's Pirate Shanty

(Attributed to the dread pirate Captain Luke Lamprey)

Sung to the air of 'Blow the Man Down'

There was a brave pirate ship set out to sea

Howl wind, bellow and growl

And the name of that ship was *The Menagerie*

With a bark and a squawk, a bellow and growl

The sails were all set and with stars as our guide

Howl wind, bellow and growl

To the Indian Ocean we sailed at high tide

With a bark and a squawk, a bellow and growl

Each cannon was manned by a hoof or a claw

Howl wind, bellow and growl

In the dead of the night, you could hear her crew call

With a bark and a squawk, a bellow and growl

The first mate was a moose and the helmsman a bear

Howl wind, bellow and growl

In the crow's nest a crocodile peeped through the air

With a bark and a squawk, a bellow and growl

We stole from the Sultan, a ruby renowned

Howl wind, bellow and growl

And hid it away where it will not be found

With a bark and a squawk, a bellow and growl

My animals guard it, the ruby so fair

Howl wind, bellow and growl

If you should seek it, you'd better beware

Of the barks and the squawks, the bellows and growls

The Waxies' Dargle (*Traditional*)

Says my aul' wan to your aul' wan
'Will ye go to the Waxies' Dargle?'
Says your aul' wan to my aul' wan
'I haven't got a farthing;
I went up to Monto town to see Uncle McArdle
But he wouldn't give me a half a crown
For to go to the Waxies' Dargle'.

Says my aul' wan to your aul' wan
'Will ye go to the Galway races?'
Says your aul' wan to my aul' wan
'I'll hawk me aul' man's braces
I went up to Capel Street to see the moneylenders
But he wouldn't give me a couple of bob
For the aul' man's red suspenders'.

Says my aul' wan to your aul' wan
'We got no beef or mutton
If we went up to Monto town

We might get a drink for nuttin"
Here's a nice piece of advice I got from an aul' fish-
   monger
'When food is scarce and you see the hearse
You'll know you've died of hunger.'

ACKNOWLEDGEMENTS

Thanks to Helen Carr, my amazing editor; to Sarah Webb for her friendship and enthusiasm; to our esteemed Laureate na nÓg, Patricia Forde, for improving beyond measure a scene that shall remain nameless; and speaking of Trishes, thanks to Trish Hennessy and the whole crew at Halfway Up The Stairs, Greystones, Co. Wicklow – *the* best children's bookshop!; to Souvik Ghosh for the lowdown on all things India; to Lily Pickle Joni Nolan for the long walks and thinking time; to the fabulously talented Shane Cluskey for his amazing illustrations; to designer extraordinaire Emma; to Ivan, Kunak, Ruth, Chloe and all my pals at The O'Brien Press (I'm still so sorry for mis-identifying Charles Dickens as Benjamin Disraeli); to my bould *Menagerie* shipmates Ian, Paul, Darragh and Ronan – Yarrr, me hearties!; to my long-suffering family, thanks again for putting up with all me aul guff; and, lastly, thanks to the mighty Eoin Colfer, whose beard is the envy of many and an inspiration to us all.